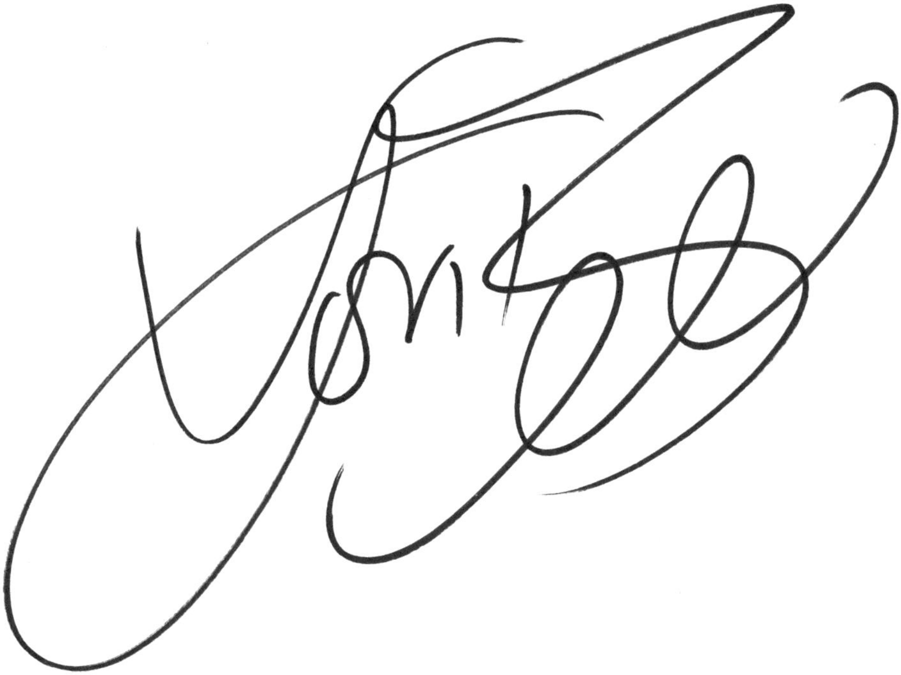

Consequences

Book 3

Orion Lane Trilogy

Lori Bell

This book is a work of fiction. Names, characters, places, and incidents are the product of the author's imagination or are used fictitiously. Any resemblance to actual events, locales, or persons, living or dead, is coincidental.

Copyright © 2020 by Lori Bell

All rights reserved. This book or any portion thereof may not be reproduced or used in any manner whatsoever without the express written permission of the publisher except for the use of brief quotations in a book review.

Cover photograph by CanStock Photo

Printed by Kindle Direct Publishing

ISBN 9798561717703

DEDICATION

Be accountable to yourself in this world. Own your life. Your failures should be because you made the choice, not anyone else deciding anything for you.

Chapter 1

A keen sense of right and wrong never failed to guide her throughout her life. Until Winnie crossed paths with Milo Brand. He changed her in ways she wasn't proud of, but in times of weakness and desperation Winnie believed she had merely chosen survival.

Despite how she had gripped Baylor's arm and stalled him when they were standing on the pier above the Edenton Bay that Milo had fallen into, Winnie ultimately didn't want him to drown.

She watched Baylor jump off the pier and into the water where Milo was submerged. Winnie's heart raced when Baylor surfaced with Milo. Baylor cupped the palm of his hand in a pistol grip underneath Milo's chin to keep both his nose and mouth above water. He managed to tow Milo closer to the pier, where Winnie was down on her knees near the edge. Baylor didn't waste a second, frantically telling her what to do. "Grab ahold of him and pull, and I will boost him up. Count of three! One, two…"

Winnie tugged with all she had, tightening her grip around him. He was limp, deadweight. If it weren't for Baylor's strength and ability to hoist Milo's body up from the water, Winnie's effort would have been useless.

She managed to flatten Milo on his back, but his legs still hung down in the water. Once Baylor lifted himself out of the bay and onto the pier, he swung Milo's legs up and out of the water.

Everything had happened so fast. Winnie's husband caught her and Baylor in each other's arms out there on the waterfront. He was enraged. Heated words were exchanged. Threats were made. Baylor feared that Winnie believed she would have no choice but to go back to her husband. Winnie knew without a doubt that she would lose her daughter if she ever left Milo. Her affair with Baylor would now have to end. She despised Milo and she wanted to be free of him. When he stumbled and fell off the pier and into the water, for a moment she wished he would drown and be gone from her life forever.

She and Baylor were both down on their knees. Neither one of them could find a pulse on his body. *Milo wasn't breathing.* Winnie saw the panic in Baylor's eyes. He began the rescue breathing. She called 911.

Winnie pressed the phone to her ear as she watched Baylor force air into Milo's airway every few seconds. Three attempts later, Milo's body jerked as he began to cough and eventually heave water. Baylor forced him to turn over on his side. He violently coughed and sputtered until he regained the ability to take a complete breath on his own. It was terrifying to witness.

CONSEQUENCES

Sirens were approaching Orion Lane. Baylor backed off, as his job was done. He pulled the man out of the water and revived him. Winnie stayed near Milo's side. "Take it easy. Slow, deep breaths. The paramedics are on their way." Milo stared blankly at her as she spoke to him. He was pale and lethargic. Baylor stood in the middle of the pier as the paramedics rushed to them.

They were able to fill in the blanks. *He stumbled and fell off the pier. He was not the strongest swimmer. He recently recovered from a spinal cord injury. They estimated that he was submerged underwater for a couple minutes before Baylor was able to pull him up.*

Baylor drove behind the ambulance, as Winnie was subdued in the passenger seat beside him. Oakley had returned from her jog with Adler in the stroller just as the paramedics were loading up Milo into the ambulance on a gurney. Oakley stayed behind with the baby so Winnie could go to the hospital. Baylor wanted to drive her, despite her objections. *Milo was furious with them for being together.*

The paramedics noted that Milo had a lot of water in his lungs. They were also concerned about his rapid heart rate, lethargy, and previous spinal cord injury. There was no question that Milo needed to be examined by a healthcare professional. Winnie wanted to feel grateful, knowing that he was going to be okay, but she didn't want to stand by his side at the hospital and identify herself as his wife. It pained her to think about what was going to happen to her life now that Milo knew she was having an affair with Baylor. Her greatest fear was that he would hold true to his threat and take her child away.

"I know it doesn't seem like it now, but we will get through this," Baylor told her as he pulled into a parking space on the hospital grounds. They needed a moment alone together in his truck before Winnie went into the hospital. Neither one of them wanted to speculate if she would be going home with Milo once he was released. Winnie only braced herself for whatever fallout Milo would unleash on her.

"You should go," she told him. "Just drop me off here."

"I can at least wait to see what the doctor says. I'll stay out here if you don't want me to go inside with you."

"I would like nothing more than for you to be by my side in there," Winnie told him, "but we both know we can't."

Baylor nodded his head. He would still wait for her though. She didn't have to agree to that. "Don't go back to him, Win. Please don't."

Her eyes clouded with tears as she turned in her seat to face him beside her. He had quickly changed out of his wet clothes before they left, but his hair was still damp.

"Do you really think I have a choice?"

"Yes, I do."

Winnie instantly felt offensive. "I am a mother. You don't understand. You're not a parent. I can't give up my baby. I won't abandon her. Not for anything… not even for us, Baylor." She choked on a sob, and Baylor reached for her. He held her face in his hands.

"I would never ask you to choose; not like that," he looked at her directly in the eyes. "You know me better than that. I am only saying that you have rights. You can fight that bastard."

"He doesn't play fair!" Winnie reacted.

"He's scum, but he's not above the law. Trust me. Just hire a lawyer."

"I held you back…"

"What?"

"On the pier, after Milo fell in the water, I gripped your arm. Why do you think I did that?"

Baylor shrugged. "It was a moment of panic and disbelief. I don't know. I wanted you to be safe on the pier, so I knew I had to go in after him. What are you getting at, Winnie?"

"You should have let him drown. My mind went there, to that dark place, when I saw Milo struggling in the water. He couldn't stay afloat. I thought of what my life, our lives, would be like if he were gone forever."

Baylor's eyes were wide. "You are still reeling from the shock of everything. Milo caught us out there. He realized we're together. Then, he fell in the water and you were scared and not thinking clearly." Winnie backed away from his touch. She shook her head multiple times in protest, and Baylor wanted no part of her nonsense. "The Winnie that I know and love with all my heart is a woman who would never be willing to compromise who she is or what feels right — not for anyone or anything. If the only way to win was by breaking all the rules, you would rather lose. Tell me that isn't true. Look at me and admit that you would have been able to live with yourself if we had let Milo die out there."

"I can't."

"You can't what?"

"I can't say that's true. I'm not the same person anymore. Milo has changed me. Weakness and desperation have won." Winnie placed two fingers on the door handle.

"Stop!" Baylor raised his voice. She wasn't startled. She wasn't taken aback or afraid. She could see the despair in his eyes. Baylor refused to believe that Winnie didn't have any fight left anymore. "Don't you see that this is what he wants? He wants an obedient woman. He throws threats around and makes demands and in return he gets some strange kind of thrill out of watching you be submissive to him. Yes, you are the mother of his child — but your heart never belonged to him. Go. Make sure he knows that."

Winnie turned away from him, so he would not see the tears streaming down her face. She opened the truck door and stepped down. The moment her feet touched the ground, her knees felt weak. The strong-willed woman that Baylor spoke of was a long way away. She pushed the door closed behind her and forced herself not to look back at him. As she put one foot in front of the other, Winnie desperately tried not to focus on how she was once again walking away from Baylor to sink back into a falsified life with Milo.

Chapter 2

Winnie stood outside the hospital room where she was told she could find her husband. All she could think about was Adler. She wanted to dial Oakley's number and tell her to keep her baby safe. For no reason, should she let anyone take her. Winnie's memory flashed to the time that Milo's father had stepped into the beach house, unbeknownst to her, and carried Adler into another room. In an instant, she was gone. That had been Milo's warning to Winnie then. His words still terrified her.

Any moment she can vanish. I'll know where she is, of course. I am her father. She adores me. I can give her a very good life, the best of everything. I do, however, prefer to continue to give our baby her mother. That's up to you, of course.

Winnie opened the door. Milo was alone and awake and staring back at her the moment she entered the hospital room.

CONSEQUENCES

"We seem to be making this a habit," he spoke first, and his voice was strong. It amazed her how quickly that man could bounce back from trauma. "First the shooting at the bank left me hospitalized and then you supposedly had an eating disorder." It was hurtful how he continued to write off her problem as if it meant nothing at all. "And now, this."

"The doctor says you're going to be fine, Milo," Winnie half-heartedly stated. *Thanks to Baylor saving your life,* she thought, but refrained from saying those words aloud.

"Right. The sooner I get out of here, the better. I really would rather not spend the night here. I want to be home, in my own bed." Winnie felt a chill behind his words.

"You almost died, Milo. Let the doctors be sure you're okay." She was hoping for some borrowed time; she at least wanted one night.

"I'd rather talk about what happened before I fell off the pier and into the water." Winnie stayed silent. "We've made a mess of things, Wynette. We're married, but we're not acting like it anymore. I've made mistakes...and so have you."

Baylor was not a mistake.

"We need to regain our focus on what's important and that's our marriage and our family." Milo was strangely calm; unlike how he acted on the pier when he realized she and Baylor were together.

"I don't understand how you cannot see it." Suddenly she embodied courage under fire. "We are not good for each other.

Milo, you can have any woman you want." Although, she thought to herself how she wouldn't wish on anyone else the way he treated her. The destructive, manic, back-and-forth behavior had taken its toll.

"I chose you," he responded, as if he wasn't affected by her blunt words. "I wanted you from the first moment I saw you, and I knew you were going to be my wife. What you said is untrue. You absolutely are good for me. I need you. I want your goodness and purity to make me a better man."

A wife who had an affair with another man was hardly a model of goodness and purity, but Winnie was not about to throw that back in his face. "I can't be who you want me to be." Winnie's therapist helped her to see that she had allowed her husband to get inside her mind and negatively influence her time and again. Their relationship was unhealthy from the beginning.

"That's where you're wrong. You just need to be willing. You're a Brand now. Enjoy the perks that money and prestige can offer you, and what I can give you. Forget the lake life, or any misguided fantasies you've had there." Milo referred to Baylor. He could not have been more wrong. The life Winnie could have with Baylor was the only one she ever truly wanted.

"Cutting me off, from the only life I knew before you, certainly is not the way to make me happy, Milo."

"Right. We've been over this. The thing about that was, I thought you had some type of corny sentimental connection to the water or the property. I had no idea that you were all in with Baylor Graham."

She watched her husband clench his jaw and once again she kept quiet. She would not defend the love that she shared with Baylor or the relationship they have nurtured. Milo had no right to know anything more.

"So, tell me," Milo continued, "what would be the way to make you happy?"

Winnie stared blankly at him. She had no words. Well, she had the words in the forefront of her mind, but she did not say that getting a divorce and being free to start a life with Baylor and Adler was all she wanted. "That's a rhetorical question," she finally spoke. "I believe you already know what I want. I want you to set me free. Co-parent Adler with me, but let's agree that being married isn't good for either of us or for our daughter."

Milo smirked. It was the cocky look that he wore on his face whenever he had the upper hand. It unnerved Winnie every time. "I think you may need to be reminded that you are free to go, Wynette. I am not preventing you from filing for a divorce. Just understand that there will be no joint custody or co-parenting, as you phrased it. The court will honor the document that you signed, leaving your daughter to me until she's officially an adult. That would be some 18th birthday party for her, wouldn't it? 'Adler, look, there's your mother; the one you haven't seen for your entire childhood; the woman who abandoned you out of pure selfishness.'"

His words sickened her. She was stuck. Baylor was wrong. There was no way out of this marriage. It wouldn't matter if she hired her own lawyer, because she had already lost this fight. "You know that I would never leave my baby." Winnie's eyes were stone cold as she stared at her husband from across the room.

"It's settled then," Milo stated, clearly feeling victorious. "You've chosen me and Adler over your lover."

They were interrupted by an abrupt knock on the door before it swung open and Thomas Brand stepped in. He spoke first. Winnie had nothing to say to the man, and Milo always waited for his father to make the first move. He was like some sort of trained puppet under the control of his master.

"Son," he stepped past Winnie and went to Milo's bedside, "make this the last time you encounter a brush with death. It's getting tiresome."

"Right," Milo chuckled under his breath. Winnie watched his father hand him a cell phone from his suit coat pocket. "Thank you for replacing my phone. I'm sure my other one is at the bottom of the bay by now." Winnie hadn't thought of anything being in his possession when he fell into the water fully clothed.

Thomas turned to face Winnie. "My gratitude to you, and your friend of course, for saving my son's life."

Winnie awkwardly nodded her head in response when Milo interjected. "That's unnecessary, Dad. She's fucking him."

Thomas Brand's eyes widened, and he turned to face Milo again. "Better start laying some ground rules in your marriage."

Milo nodded in compliance, and Winnie couldn't take it anymore. She would not stand there and be treated as a worthless human being. She darted toward the door as she muttered, "I am going to check on Adler."

"No need," Thomas Brand's words stopped her. "She's in good hands."

"Excuse me?" Winnie's chest felt tight.

"I just came from the waterfront. Your other friend, the blonde girl, she's really something. A force to be reckoned with, I'd say."

"Why were you with Oakley and Adler?" Winnie could hear her own pulse pounding in her ears. This was exactly what she feared earlier. *Had it been a premonition?*

She wanted to slap the smirk off his face. *Like father, like son.* "I offered to take my granddaughter off her hands, but your beautiful friend made it clear that I was trespassing and demanded that I leave her property."

Milo and Thomas shared a chuckle, which was the last thing Winnie heard as she bolted out the door of the hospital room and into the hallway. She had her phone in her hand and sent a call to Oakley within a matter of seconds.

"Tell me that Adler is safe with you!" Winnie could hear the panic in her own voice when Oakley answered.

"She's fine. I'm holding her in my arms right now. I guess you know the arrogant patriarch was here. Regardless, I would never let anything happen to Adler."

Winnie was finally able to breathe. "I know that. It's them I don't trust."

"What's happening there?"

"Milo is fine, I think. I don't even know what the doctor said after he checked him out. Oak, I have to stay with him. He's not going to let me out of our marriage without sacrificing my baby. Baylor and I will be forced to be apart. My life is over in so many ways." Winnie choked on a sob.

"Hey," Oakley's heart broke for her, "don't completely give up hope. There must be a way. I mean, you might have to abide by this craziness for a little while longer, but—"

"I wish he had drowned." There. She said it again. "There was a moment on the pier when I held Baylor back from going in the water to save Milo." Winnie kept her voice low on the phone as she walked farther down the hospital corridor.

"Oh my God…" Oakley reacted.

"I know," Winnie was aware how wrong that was, "but look at what's happening now. Milo knows about me and Baylor. This feels like a game changer. He's going to play the Adler card for everything now. I had my freedom before, but now he doesn't trust me."

"I understand wishing the man dead," Oakley admitted, "but that's not who you are."

"Now you sound like Baylor."

"We only want you to see that by staying with him you are accepting defeat."

"No. Defeat, for me, would be watching him take my daughter from my arms and knowing that he was never going to give her back to me. I have this vision of her little arms reaching for me, she's crying out for me, and I am not able to get to her." Tears were rolling down Winnie's face as she pressed her back against a wall near an exit. "I tell myself that I can live with anything else — anything but that. I would not survive losing my baby."

Chapter 3

Immediately after she ended the call with Oakley, her phone buzzed. Winnie was hesitant to answer because she was purposely avoiding him now.

"Milo?" Winnie remained stationary at the end of the hallway.

"Where are you?"

"I'm still here in the hospital. Is your father gone?"

"He left when the doctor came in."

"What did the doctor have to say?"

"There's excess fluid on my lungs. I'm having a procedure to remove it today, which means I can't be discharged until tomorrow." Winnie felt a wave of relief knowing that she didn't have stay at the beach house with him tonight. She kept silent on the opposite end of the phone. "Winnie, are you still there?"

"I'm here."

CONSEQUENCES

"Could you just make your way back to my room? It seems silly to talk to you by phone when we're under the same roof."

"I need to pick up Adler," she instantly made an excuse. "I will be back for you tomorrow." She ended their call and shoved her phone in the pocket of her jeans. She was certain that Milo would send her multiple texts or call her again, but right now she simply didn't care. She glanced outside, through the glass door. She noticed his truck earlier and had known that he never left. It touched her to know that Baylor was still waiting for her. Winnie pushed open the door to go to him.

He watched her walk through the parking lot until she reached his truck and got in. "Hi," Winnie spoke first.

"Hi yourself," he smiled at her. God, that man. His brown hair was wavy and it always curled near his ears after it dried naturally. She reached over and tucked a small curl behind his right ear. "Are you going to tell me what's happening in there? Is Milo going to be alright?"

"There's some fluid on his lungs that will have to be removed. He'll stay here overnight and come home tomorrow."

"Home," Baylor stated. "What does that mean for you now?"

She momentarily turned away from him. "Milo will not agree to shared custody if I divorce him. He continues to recap that the agreement I unknowingly signed will hold up in court and I will lose Adler. And then his father showed up to make sure that I knew he was at the triplex after we left to follow the ambulance. He wanted to take Adler from Oakley."

"Are you kidding me?"

"Thank God that no one intimidates Oakley. She ordered him to leave and threatened to call the police for trespassing."

"Do you think he would have taken A.J.?"

Winnie nodded her head. "To prove a point, yes."

"Nothing changes then. Milo once again gets his way."

"I don't know if I agree that nothing changes," she stated. "Because he knows about us now, I feel like he's going to monitor my every move. He's not going to tolerate me coming back to the triplex and seeing you."

"Is that what he said?"

"He told his father in front of me not to be grateful to us for saving his life, especially not to you because you are my lover."

"I can't imagine that going over well."

"I left the room. I can't handle how those two gang-up on me."

"I don't know how you are going to react to this, but I called a lawyer for you. I want some professional advice. You can go along with me, or not. It's up to you. I just can't sit back and do nothing."

Winnie reached for him. She touched his face. "I love you for holding onto hope when there isn't much to grasp."

CONSEQUENCES

"As long as you love me, I'll always have hope for us." Baylor closed the space between them and held her.

Winnie was still in his arms when she asked him to take her back to the triplex. She didn't say, for one more night, because some things were just easier left unsaid.

When anything happened with her family members —good or bad— Sally Brand was always the first to know. She was surprised to not find Winnie at the hospital when she went to see her grandson. Sally thought about the words she and Milo exchanged as she now sat on the bench swing near her rose garden.

Milo was upset because Winnie had abruptly left him sitting alone in the hospital. *He had almost drowned for chrissakes!* Sally then asked him for the whole story, *the truth*, and now she shook her head at how complicated their young lives had become. She was lost in thought when her daughter, Remi made her way through the grass and to the swing. She sat down beside her. "You're miles away...what's going through your mind?"

"One fact at the moment," Sally answered as the warm wind further disheveled her already untamed white hair. "I'm not proud to be a Brand. I never have been. The controlling nature of your father and your brothers...and now my grandson... has only caused hurt."

"So Milo nearly drowned and you're on Winnie's side?"

Sally nodded her head. "I've always been on her side. I didn't want the two of them to get married, but I never imagined it would be this bad." Sally had explained that Milo deceived Winnie to get her pregnant, and while she married him on her own free will — she was now trapped.

This was precisely what Remi didn't miss about living in Nags Head Beach, in close proximity to her family. People needed to live their own lives without anyone else meddling. Remi couldn't have cared less if Milo was unhappy in his marriage. "Let them live their lives, Mom. If they are unhappy, they'll eventually get divorced."

Sally studied her daughter for a long moment with a smirk on her face. "Everything is just black or white for you, isn't it?" Sally knew all too well how Remi's father had lived his life very much the same. Their nearly year-long affair ended when he was eager to go off on another adventure. It was a way of life for him to drift from one place to another. He asked Sally more than once to come along. She couldn't leave her family though; and Remington Boyd had been unaware that she was pregnant with his child. Sally raised her daughter as a Brand. She was the baby sister in a family with already three boys.

Remi shrugged. "Everything is just easier that way."

"To each his own, honey. I'm not judging you."

"Right. And next you will tell me that you just want me to be happy."

"Are you?" Sally asked. "Does traveling the world and having no place to settle down make you happy?"

"Nags Head is my home, and I know it's here for me whenever I want to come back," Remi avoided the direct question.

"Well whatever brought you back to me this time, it's good to have you home."

Remi squeezed her mother's plump hand on the bench between them. She wasn't ready to delve into the details that led her home.

Chapter 4

Winnie held her baby girl in her arms as she made her way into the hospital. When they reached Milo's room, he was dressed in fresh clothes which someone else had obviously brought to him. Pleated khaki pants, an open-collared white button-down dress shirt with the sleeves rolled back to the elbows, and loafers sans socks. His jet-black hair was densely styled with product.

Milo looked as if he had been pacing when they walked in. With a point, Adler called her daddy by name. He melted each time she was in the room, in his arms, and now she could say, *Dada*. Milo went to her and lifted her from Winnie's arms. It occurred to her now that he wasn't using a cane. The fall off the pier and into the water must not have hindered the healing of his spinal cord. She kept quiet and heard him tell Adler that he missed her so much as he gave her multiple kisses on her full cheeks. Her features, dark hair, dark eyes, and porcelain skin were striking. She was a beautiful baby girl who adored her daddy. Winnie couldn't deny that.

"You look ready. Did the doctor release you?" Winnie spoke as if she cared.

"Yes, I'm good. Definitely ready to put this behind me." Winnie watched him carry Adler over to the bed where he put a leather bag on his shoulder, and then the three of them left together.

The drive from Edenton to Nags Head Beach was forty minutes. Winnie looked in the rearview mirror as she drove with Milo in the passenger seat beside her. Adler had fallen asleep, and Milo's full attention was now going to be on her.

"So, you and Adler stayed at the triplex last night?"

She nodded. *What did he expect her to say?* She wasn't about to confirm his suspicions that Baylor had stayed with them.

"I'm not looking back, and I don't want you to either. Onward from here, Wynette. Forget the angry words and the threats out on that pier. I was caught off guard, but I've had some time to rethink it all." Now more than ever, Milo wanted to reclaim what was his.

"But the threat still remains for you to take my daughter from me if I want out of this marriage?" Winnie called him out on his effort to make peace.

He smiled and Winnie forced her eyes back on the open road as she heard him say, "That's correct."

Oakley sat behind Jack's executive desk at Harper Publishing. She continued to commute for the one-hour drive from Edenton, North Carolina to Norfolk, Virginia whenever she had to fulfill obligations there. Her first book, *Blindsided* was a smashing success, as it remained on the New York Times bestsellers list for several consecutive weeks. And now her readers eagerly awaited the sequel.

Jack was tied up in a meeting, but he assured her that he would be finished in time to go with her to the book signing at a quaint little bookstore downtown Norfolk. Oakley attempted to make good use of her time, writing. She stared at the computer screen as she clicked on the blinking cursor at the bottom of the page. She hovered the mouse overtop the text before she selected the entire page that she had just written — and then she deleted it. This story was only halfway finished. She knew Jack was eager to take a look at what she had written so far. But it still unnerved her how her first book was published after Jack had tweaked and edited so much of the story that Oakley felt as if she was deceiving her readers, because she didn't feel like the sole author.

She was distracted now, and her words weren't flowing on the page. She stood up to stretch her legs in her 3-inch heels. She tugged on the hem of her short red skirt and smoothed the front of it with her palms. She walked over to a mirror that hung above the sofa in Jack's office. She ran her fingers through her long blonde hair and stared at her face. She needed to reapply her lipstick before the book signing. She found a tube in her handbag and returned to the mirror. Just as she relined her lips with color, Jack opened the door behind her. She watched in the mirror as he stepped closer to her. That fluttery feeling in her belly…and those chill bumps on her skin...were the kind of things she felt whenever he walked in the room.

Most had seen her beautiful face painted, but it was Jack who saw it flawless in the morning light. He wondered why she bothered to apply any makeup — because she didn't need it. Not in his eyes.

"You're staring," she called him out as he saw her painted lips twitch into a grin in the mirror before she spun around and put a cap on the lipstick in her hand.

"I was just thinking how lucky I'd feel to be that tube of lipstick." He could hardly wait to kiss her again. It was killing him to miss her when she was gone, and then not be able to touch her when she returned. He would wait forever for her though. That's what falling in love had done to him.

She giggled out loud. "Focus, Harper. We have work to do." She said those words nonchalantly, but there wasn't an inch of her that didn't ache to be in his arms again. She forced away the sultry image in her mind of him backing her against the wall, with her legs wrapped around his middle.

"Right," he smiled at her. "How's the book coming along?"

"Pretty good."

"Yeah? When are you going to share what you have written with me?" The deadline for the completion of the sequel was only two months away.

"When I'm ready."

He nodded. "Let's be clear about something. This trip out, you're not leaving until I read what you have finished. And don't tell me it's too raw and sloppy. I've seen it all. And before you object, don't. What happens or does not happen between us is all on you. I will be patient for as long as you need me to, because you are the only woman for me." He could see in her eyes that she wanted to smile. "But Harper Publishing calls the shots with your books."

"You mean you do," Oakley corrected him, and he subsequently winked at her.

"After the signing, we're coming back here. You can take a nap on that sofa while I dive into your story."

She glanced at that white leather sofa against the wall. "Or you could join me on the sofa? Wouldn't be the first time…"

Jack's eyes widened. "You're messing with me."

She shrugged. And he pretended her words that provoked the visual of the two of them together …naked…skin to skin…with their limbs entangled… didn't affect him.

"As I said, you're putting out later."

They laughed out loud together as he held the door and they left arm in arm. There was shared physical contact between them, hand holding and platonic touches, but they had not kissed… or made love in a very long time. Not since the day that Oakley discovered Jack had broken her trust. She had long forgiven him for altering the story in her first book, but she was afraid to fully trust him again. And the funny thing was, Oakley knew deep down in her soul that this was more about her than Jack.

All her life she was haunted by the memory of her father walking away from her when she was four years old. He packed his bags and loaded them onto the bed of his pickup truck. Oakley recalled how her mother was done begging and pleading. She had already cried her last tear for him. When she wiggled out of her mother's arms to run after her daddy, he only kept walking. All she saw was his back as she called after him and he never turned around.

When Oakley was six years old, her mother remarried, and the man who became Oakley's stepfather adopted her and raised her as his own. From then on, she was a Marks, and she swore to herself that her birthfather no longer mattered. Even still, the pain of being abandoned had deeply scarred her. Her ability to trust was based on a foundation of shaky ground, so Oakley didn't let people into her heart very easily. Not since she, Baylor, and Winnie all became renters at the triplex on Orion Lane had she allowed herself to love so unconditionally. And then she met Jack. He held the master key to her dream. Because of him, she was an author now. Jack also was the first and only man she had ever truly fallen in love with — but she didn't know how to allow herself to trust him with her whole heart.

There was a never-ending line of people that zig-zagged through the bookstore for the Oakley Marks signing. Someone mentioned how the line extended outside onto the sidewalk. Oakley greeted her readers, took photographs with many of them, and signed their books. It still felt surreal that her book was in their hands.

The smile across Oakley's face was genuine as she asked each reader their name and gave everyone ample attention before she signed their book. A security guard stood to her left, and Jack was on the other side of him. An employee at the bookstore managed the line and kept it moving. There were mostly women there to see her, but a few men showed up with books to be signed for their wives or girlfriends. They were careful to clarify not being a romance novel reader, which made Oakley laugh.

A young girl in line, who was probably all of nineteen years old, asked Oakley for a hug. Oakley stood up, completely willing. As she embraced the girl, Oakley glanced over her shoulder and saw a man waiting in line. He held a book in his hand and was looking down when Oakley spotted him. She didn't understand why he had come back again. Jack gave him a stern warning in the lobby of Harper Publishing months ago when he showed up unannounced to see Oakley. Her heart raced. Her hands trembled. She didn't want to draw any negative attention to herself in front of all those people. They were her readers who had come to see her. *What was her father doing there?* Oakley glanced at her security guard. All she had to do was make eye contact with him. Their safe word in public was bookmark. She would mouth it to him, or simply say it aloud, and then he would discreetly remove her father from the line.

But Oakley was unable to get his attention. He and Jack were sharing a conversation and both were oblivious to how unsettled she felt. The line was shrinking, and he was getting closer. They made eye contact. The man still carried himself with more confidence than arrogance. He was 54 years old now, but when Oakley looked at him, she still saw a 30-year-old man. She clearly saw herself in him. She had his eyes, nose, and square chin.

Oakley didn't want him to move any closer to her. She spun her head around to get Jack's attention. And this time she had it. She watched him bump arms with the security guard to bring his attention to Oakley was well. She knew she looked panicked. The reader in front of her was talking and she had not heard a single word.

She was supposed to say... *bookmark*... but that word never formed on her lips. She finally made direct eye contact with Jack and mouthed the words, *he's here.*

In a split second, Jack strained his neck to look past Oakley and at the line of people. "Get him out of here. Fourth guy down the line. Plaid shirt. Grayish hair." Jack's words were directed at the security guard.

"Excuse me." Oakley turned away from the person in line who was waiting for an autograph. "Jack!" she stopped both him and the security guard.

She had his attention. He stood close to her. The panic in her eyes alarmed him. He didn't want that man anywhere near her. Why had he shown up again? It was downright creepy the way he was standing in line among the readers as if he needed to find a way to hoard a moment of Oakley's attention.

Oakley spoke in no uncertain terms. "Remove him from the line, but hold him. I want to talk to him privately after the signing."

Jack objected. "No, Oak. That's not a smart idea."

"Now is not the time to get into this. Don't make a scene. Jack, you know as well as I do that this could bring us negative publicity if it gets out. I don't want anyone to associate him with me. Just tell him to wait."

Chapter 5

The last of her fans had gone through the signing line. There was a storage area in the back of the bookstore, which was where Jack told Oakley her father was waiting.

"Are you sure you want to do this?" Jack did not want to let her confront her long, lost father alone.

Oakley paused before she answered him. Of course she was uncertain. He was missing for her entire lifetime. She was over that loss, or so she had told herself time and again. Confronting him now was for the sole purpose of making it clear to him that showing up unwelcomed was unacceptable. And he would never again be a part of her life. *He lost his chance.*

"Jack," she wanted to explain this to him, but she suddenly was overcome with emotion. Her eyes teared up and her voice caught in her throat. He reached for her hand and gently squeezed it while she continued to speak. "I can't handle this; knowing I will have to look over my shoulder everywhere I go in fear of seeing him just turn up again. What does he want from me? I need to know."

Jack nodded. "Okay. I'll go with you."

"No."

He exhaled a frustrated sigh. "You're the most stubborn woman in the entire world." *But he loved her.* "I'm sending security with you then."

"Just be right outside the door. You'll know if I need you."

Jack pulled her close and gently pressed his lips to her forehead. Oakley closed her eyes and allowed that moment with him to fuel her with the strength to face the first man in her life who broke her little 4-year-old heart.

She closed the door behind her. The open storage area had concrete flooring and the echo of her 3-inch heels bounced off the farthest wall. He had been sitting on the edge of an old desk with books piled high around him. He stood when he saw her.

She left at least ten feet of distance between them. It simultaneously pained her and awed her to look at him. He was older, yet unfazed by Father Time in most ways.

"Oakley," he spoke her name, and it was uncanny to her again to realize she had not forgotten the sound of his voice. "Thank you for seeing me."

CONSEQUENCES

"You keep showing up," she spoke with little emotion. "Do you know that I used to pray in my bed at night, no, I would get out of the bed once my mother had tucked me in, and I would drop to my knees and beg God to bring you back home. I was so sure that you still wanted me." The memory of that threatened to bring tears to her eyes, but she wouldn't let him see her cry. He didn't deserve that kind of emotion from her. "Decades have gone by. Why now? I want to know what you could possibly want from me after all this time."

He cleared his throat as a stall tactic, a pause, before he found the courage to give her an answer she deserved. "What I want, is for you to know that I'm proud of you."

She shrugged. "I won the elementary school spelling bee when I was in the second grade. I was president of the Student Council in junior high, and in high school I was crowned the Homecoming queen. Where was your pride then? That's when it mattered. Not now." *And not ever again.*

Her father nodded his head in agreement. "I understand that I caused you a lot of pain. I'm not here to dredge that up for you. That wasn't my intention. As I said, I feel proud to know who you've become. I used to look at you and say that you were too perfect to come from me."

Emotion filled her chest. "Why did you leave?" She gave up asking her mother for that explanation when she was a child, because she merely offered the same answer every time. *He loved them, but could no longer stay.*

"I couldn't be who you needed me to be."

Suppressed far back in her memory were piggyback rides, fishing off the dock, butterfly kisses, and strong, loving arms that held her close. *He couldn't be who she needed him to be?*

"Do you know what I needed from you?" she asked him. "I needed you to turn around when I called your name that day. I needed to know that you still loved me… and wanted me."

"The last image I had of you was your little self on your knees on the rocks, crying, and calling after me. How does a man live with himself after that?" A life of drugs, alcohol, and meaningless women sometimes numbed the pain and disappointment.

"You tell me," she insisted.

"I don't know. I haven't been able to figure that out yet," he admitted, and Oakley realized her forthrightness came from him. "I let you down, and I'm sorry. I guess I just wanted the chance to see you again, to know that you are doing alright. And goodness gracious look at you — you are a beautiful, confident, and incredibly successful woman. A little girl whose wishes all came true, I'd say."

She instantly rejected his words. "All of my wishes? Every birthday I blew out those candles with one wish, the same wish, that didn't come true because you never came back to me. When you left me, you wrecked my ability to trust. I don't know my way around my own feelings because of you. I'm so afraid that I will not be able to handle anyone else's abandonment again. And, deep down, I fear that I will one day do the same thing to someone that I love." Other than the effortless friendship and unconditional love that she shared with Winnie and Baylor,

CONSEQUENCES

Oakley had never allowed anyone else to get that close. Not until Jack had unexpectedly made his way into her heart, while she continued to question her ability to commit to him.

Her father shook his head. He didn't want to believe it was true. "You're stronger than that, Oakley Monica." Her name was special, and no one else understood its significance the way her father did. His own mother died when he was just a child and her name was Monica. Oakley now carried on her memory, as her namesake.

Again, she rebuffed him. "I don't want your praise or anything from you anymore, but I at least deserve to know the truth. That much you owe me."

Her father wore a look of disbelief before he finally spoke. "I find it impossible to think that my headstrong daughter never sought those answers before."

"My mother's response was supposed to be enough for me. She said that you loved us, but you couldn't stay."

"I did love you," he responded, "and she was the one who forced me to go."

"I don't believe you," Oakley tried to stay calm.

"Ask her. Confront her about what went down before she kicked me out of your life."

Oakley shook her head, refusing to hear those lies from him. "I remember her crying while she begged you not to leave us."

"I don't," he stated, "or maybe that was just the show she put on for you." Oakley saw something change with his demeanor.

"I won't listen to any more of this from you!" She raised her voice and the storage room door opened. Jack and her security guard both shared the space in that doorway. Neither of them spoke a word; they only made their presence known.

"We're finished here," Oakley spoke as a matter of fact.

"Are we?" her father questioned her, and Oakley didn't like his tone.

"Don't make this about my mother. She's not the one who walked out on me. You were a grown man. If you wanted to be a father to me, no one should have been able to stop you. Only a coward would make excuses or place the blame on someone else." Oakley turned and walked away. This time, she didn't look back when her father called after her.

Jack met her midway. He secured his arm around her back to hold her up. Her strength was remarkable, he knew that, but everyone had a breaking point.

―――――

They drove in silence. All Jack said to her was, "Talk to me when you're ready." Oakley assumed he would drive back to Harper Publishing, where her car was parked. He also had implied earlier that they would work after the signing. She rested her head back on the seat and had her eyes closed for awhile. Eventually, she realized that Jack had driven her to his condo.

"What are you doing? I thought we were working tonight, and I need my car."

"You are in no condition to work, or to drive back to Edenton."

"Then call me a driver." She was miffed, but she didn't have the energy to argue with him.

"If you want me to, I will. But, first, I think you should talk about what happened tonight."

"What are you a shrink now?"

He leaned over, undid her seatbelt for her, and grinned. "Smart ass. Go. In the house now."

She tried not to smile but she failed. Jack Harper was good for her, and she damn well knew it.

Oakley ended up on the living room sofa with one end of it reclined. Jack handed her a glass of wine a moment later.

"I have to drive home," she reminded him, but took the glass from him anyway.

"No, you don't. I was told to call a driver."

She smirked.

He sat down beside her, close enough to put his feet up with hers. They shared silence until Oakley began talking about her father.

"He told me that he was proud of me. He praised me for all I've done with my life. Such a proud father..." she took a second generous sip of her wine as that snarky attitude surfaced. Jack sat back and allowed her to speak however she needed to. She was entitled to express her emotions for a man who had hurt her so deeply. "He claimed that my mother made him leave. I don't believe him. And even if that were true, I told him no one can make a man abandon his little girl. I mean, come on, what kind of leverage did she have on him if that's the way it really did happen? I swear, Jack, I cannot handle knowing my mother was behind this."

"Then don't dig any deeper. Don't ask her. Sometimes what we don't know doesn't hurt us."

"I feel like I need answers, though. Don't you see why?"

"For closure?"

"For us." She turned to look at him and his face was just inches from hers. "Men never mattered to me before. They were good for one thing and afterward I kicked them out. Fleeting relationships and Oakley Marks went hand in hand. Until you."

"I feel honored," he smiled.

"I'm serious."

"I am, too. I feel privileged and flattered beyond words to have you look at me that way, to know that you want me to be your person, the man in your life and in your bed. Oak, I know I disappointed you and you felt like I broke your trust and your heart… I swear that I'll never hurt you the way your father did. I would choose dying over losing you."

CONSEQUENCES

There were tears rolling down her face. All the emotion from the time spent with her father, and now hearing Jack open his heart to her was too much to keep bottled up inside. "I feel like I can't be who you need until I fix what's broken inside of myself."

"I understand, but I do think you need to realize that you are punishing yourself for your father's behavior. The consequences of his actions and his decisions are on him. Not you. How could his leaving have anything to do with an innocent child? You are not at fault. Yes, he broke your trust, but look at the love and devotion you've found in your life since. You have a wonderful father-figure who stepped up and took care of you. You have two of the truest friends that most of us go a lifetime wishing we had found." She smiled at him. "Do you see what I'm saying, what I'm getting at here?"

"You forgot someone," she told him, and suddenly he fell silent and waited for her to say more. "You, Jack. I've said that you held the key to making my dream come true…I'm a published author. But that key has opened so much more. My heart. It's yours, Jack. I want you to have it forever."

"Is this the wine talking?" he teased as he took her empty glass from her and placed it on the sofa beside him. "Are you sure, because I'm ready, I'm so ready to—"

"To what, Jack?"

"I think we should say it together," he told her as she touched his face with both of her hands.

"I do, too." The tears were clouding her eyes again, but she forced them away because nothing was going to hinder this moment.

"Ready?" he asked her. She nodded.

And together, they spoke the words, "I love you."

Oakley leaned in first. She made the first move to press her lips to his and their worlds collided just like the first time they shared a passionate kiss. It was intoxicating, and their desire quickly intensified. Eventually, Jack pulled away first. Her face was inches from his when he spoke. "I have a confession to make... I don't think I could have waited for you forever. It would have slowly and painfully killed me. He gestured down to his lap, to the tightness between his legs. Oakley suppressed a giggle.

She placed her hand on the bulge in his pants and she kissed him hard on the mouth when he heard her say, "you and me both."

They went upstairs to his bedroom.

They stood close in the dark, removing each other's clothing and savoring how it felt to see and touch each other again.

He laid her down on the bed and took his time exploring every inch of her body. She did the same for him.

"I've never wanted you more, Jack," she whispered in his ear, and neither one of them could wait any longer to consummate their love — again.

Chapter 6

"How are you, honey?" Sally caught Winnie's attention as she sprayed furniture polish on the surface of the coffee table in the living room and then bent to her knees to wipe it down with a dust cloth.

Winnie looked at Sally sitting on the sofa directly in front of her. It was rare that someone could have so much to say with their eyes. They were bright, and she was sharp, and fun, and worldly, and a live wire. Winnie's love and admiration for Sally saw no boundaries. The two of them shared an honest connection. Sally was one of the first residents of Nags Head Beach who hired Winnie as a caretaker, specifically to clean her house. Through the years they had grown close, and eventually they became family when Winnie married Sally's grandson.

"Miserable," she answered. "We go about our lives pretending day and night like everything is okay. Adler is thriving — she's happy and healthy and truly the only thing that keeps me going right now."

"Have you seen Baylor?"

"No, but we talk every day. He sought legal advice for me. His hopes were crushed when the lawyer told him that the document I signed would likely hold up in court and it could take years to fight a custody battle, all while Milo would be given sole custody."

Sally shook her head. "I certainly understand feeling miserable," she stated, "but I'm not one to accept defeat — and I don't want you to either."

"Easier said than done," Winnie took her frustration out on rubbing the rag onto the table in a circular motion. "It just makes me sick to my stomach the way Milo has manipulated me more than once."

Sally took a long look at Winnie. She was at least 30 pounds lighter than she had been for many years. Being bulimic had drastically changed her body. Living under such stress with Milo again had worried Sally. "You're not physically making yourself purge again, are you?"

Winnie made fleeting eye contact with Sally.

"For crying out loud, stop wiping down that table! There's going to be nothing left of it."

CONSEQUENCES

Winnie looked down and released the dust cloth from her hand. "I'm telling you, I'm a nervous wreck."

"You didn't answer my question. Have you turned back to that unhealthy and harmful way to treat your body?"

"It's a struggle. Some days are better than others, but I'm making it. My therapist wants me to text her day or night if I feel like I'm freefalling. I know that I must take good care of myself for Adler. I'm trying, Sally. I really am."

Sally nodded. "I believe you. I'm also here for you anytime, honey. You know that."

They were interrupted when Remi bounced through the doorway holding Adler on her hip. She had taken her out to see the rose garden. "Hey!" Remi's voice was loud and demanded attention in any room. Winnie smiled as her command for attention reminded her of Oakley. "I hope you don't mind, Winnie, but I took the most adorable selfie with Adler, and I posted it on my Facebook page."

"Not at all," Winnie smiled.

"Well, there's more," Remi added, "I may have claimed her as my own to throw off a few friends who haven't seen me in awhile."

Winnie and Sally laughed out loud in unison. "Now how in the world would that even be possible given you have to have sex to make a baby," Sally noted, and Winnie watched Remi roll her eyes.

"Right, mother. I'm still a virgin."

Winnie laughed under her breath and Sally shook her head at her gorgeous daughter. The girl who looked nothing like the rest of them. Her brothers all had dark hair and green eyes, and Remi was the blonde, blue-eyed beauty.

"I need to give Adler back for awhile; I have to run out," Remi noted.

"Anywhere fun?" Sally inquired.

"I don't exactly think meeting my brothers at the bank to discuss my shares would be classified as fun, but a girl has to keep tabs on her money." Remi never worked a day in her life. She earned a chemical engineering degree in college, but did not pursue a career. She lived entirely off her share of the Brand fortune.

"You betcha. Give the boys my love." Sally was proud of all her children. She didn't always agree with their choices. She spoke up. She meddled. And most times it never mattered as the Brands were all strong-willed with minds of their own.

Her brother, Thomas wrapped her in a close hug the moment she stepped into his office unannounced. "Why am I first seeing you now?" he asked her. "Haven't you been back for a couple of weeks or something?"

"Careful. I'm staying at the homestead, so you are freely admitting to never visiting our mother."

"Right," he chuckled. "How's that going for you?"

"Well. Today she implied that I must still be a virgin."

"Oh God," Thomas waved off her words. "Don't. I can't. You're our baby sis."

Remi laughed.

"Listen, it's just me today. Your other two least favorite brothers are out. You can sit and make yourself comfortable in here or grab a coffee in the lobby. I need to make an important call before we get started."

"Is Milo in?" She thought of showing him the selfie she just took with Adler.

"He is." Thomas' phone rang in the pocket of his suit jacket and he hurried to reached for it.

"Take that call," Remi told her eldest brother, "and I'll be back."

Unannounced again, Remi turned the handle and pushed open the door to Milo's office. His back was to her. He stood facing a large window with open blinds. His phone was pressed to his ear and his voice sounded agitated and demanding. She was about to take a few steps backward and leave. He didn't know she was there, and she felt awkward interrupting him. But his words immediately caught her attention.

"We have a problem. Three hundred million dollars is suddenly missing from our offshore account. I want an explanation and I want the money back in that account. You have 24 hours to straighten the fuck out of this!"

Remi abruptly backed out of his office. She left the door slightly ajar to still be able to hear what her nephew was saying. Her heart raced at the thought of what she just heard. Remi wasn't naïve. She was practically born street smart, as she grew up alongside three older brothers. Then, she traveled much of the world and had been acquainted with all types of people in all walks of life. It didn't take much for her to suspect that the Brand's family-owned bank was somehow involved in fraudulent activity. Why did they have undercover offshore accounts? Was her family scheming illegally with hundreds of millions of dollars? Dealing with that kind of money didn't exactly add up for a bank in a town with a population of less than 3,000 people.

She could hardly catch her breath. The Brand family name would forever be tarnished if they were involved in criminal activity. Remi suddenly wanted no part of her bank shares. Cashing in on illegal funds would make her as guilty as the rest of them. *Her brothers. Her nephew.* My God, she needed to get out of there. And suddenly she again wanted to be as far away from Nags Head Beach as possible.

Chapter 7

Secrets. Did they always have a way of coming out? What if the problem fixed itself; if the recipient of Milo's demands found the glitch and life resumed as it was? Remi didn't want this on her shoulders. She lived her life free of family drama and complications. Coming back to Nags Head Beach was a mistake.

Then there was that day six months ago when Remi spent some time in Alabama. A friend of a friend had a vacant beach house. Remi never expected to bump into a familiar face there, but she had. Walt Seger lived across the street from the Brands in Nags Head Beach for decades. He had a wife who died suddenly in her sixties and children who never came around. Walt ended up moving away and living in a retirement community in Orange Beach. Remi bumped into him at a local pub and drank a beer with him.

They talked about the good ole days, as Walt remembered them, and Remi merely humored him by listening. None of what he recalled was worth repeating until the old man caught her attention with a story about her mother.

She put that rose garden in, and it's like it became an obsession for her. I suppose it gave her a purpose; I understand that. But I think it was more about that gardener than the roses.

Remi stopped him. She said she didn't remember having a gardener.

It was before you were born, Walt told her, and he chuckled under his breath. *There was chemistry there between the drifter and your mother.*

Remi interrupted again to clarify who the drifter was?

The gardener. He and your mother spent a lot of time together, while your brothers were in school, and your daddy was making all that money as the banker.

Sally had never mentioned having a gardener. As far back as Remi could remember, her mother handled the gardening entirely herself — and to perfection. Remi asked Walt if he knew what happened to the gardener.

As I said, he moved on. He wasn't from Nags Head. He stayed about a year and then I never saw him again. I asked Sally about him once and she appeared uncomfortable and defensive, so I dropped it.

Remi attempted to laugh off Walt's words, but he drank the last of his beer and looked her in the eye with one more thing to say.

CONSEQUENCES

You know, your brothers, those Brand boys were all look-alikes with their dark hair and dark eyes. And then you came along with blonde hair and blue eyes. Much like the gardener.

Winnie stood up and pushed her chair in. *"That's the beer talking, Walt, and it's time for me to go."*

Now, now. No need to leave in a tiff. I'm only saying what I saw. The man was a drifter. And here you are, not ready to settle anywhere either. Genetics, perhaps? Something to think about, right?

And that was what brought Remi back home to Nags Head Beach. She knew nothing about this gardener, other than what their old neighbor Walt told her.

What Remi did know for certain was all her life she had never felt like she belonged. She thought that was because she grew up with three brothers who she simply had nothing in common with because they were all considerably older than her. She made up other excuses for feeling different than everyone else in her family, but she never second guessed her life. She embraced the fact that she was a free spirit and she had the means to travel. She thought of herself as an explorer, not a drifter.

And now she was sitting on some sort of locked vault with two potential secrets hidden inside. Both were explosive and would change everything. She contemplated keeping silent. Lives would completely shatter in her entire family if there was any truth behind the bank acting as a coverup for something illegal. She couldn't be the one to expose her own family. She adored her brothers. And then there was the hearsay — this information, a clue that only her mother could provide the answer for. Uncovering either secret, if that's what those were, would only bring her family pain.

Baylor stood on the pier watching the sunset. The waterfront, and his life there, just was not the same anymore with Winnie gone and Oakley spending more time in Norfolk with Jack. He missed them and the time when they all three lived in the triplex on Orion Lane together. He especially yearned for Winnie and sharing nights like this with her.

His phone buzzed in his pocket, interrupting his loneliness. It was Winnie. "Standing on this pier in the dark night just isn't the same without you," was how he answered her call.

"I don't think I've ever been more jealous in my life!" Winnie reacted. "Actually, I take that back." She remembered all those years when he didn't see her in the same light as he did now. His girlfriend's name was Kari then, and Baylor believed that he wanted to marry her. Those envious feelings damn near destroyed Winnie. But that was in the past. Now, Baylor wanted to spend his life with her and Adler… but she was locked into her marriage with Milo.

"Yeah, there's no need to bring that up," Baylor stopped her. If only he and Winnie would have chosen each other before Milo Brand came into the picture and turned their lives upside down. "How are things going there?"

"Milo is working late," she noted. "Something is going on at the bank apparently. I don't know, I didn't ask and he didn't offer any information. He sounded agitated or distracted so we didn't talk long when he called."

CONSEQUENCES

"I wish that I wasn't forty miles away right now. I could sneak in your bedroom window and keep you company tonight," Baylor smiled into the phone.

Winnie was up for that challenge. "I've already tucked Adler in for the night, and I can't think of anything that I want more right now than to be with you."

Baylor took long, swift strides off the pier and into the grass that led up to the triplex. His phone was still against his ear. "All I have to do is grab my truck keys and I can be on my way to you in minutes. You're talking less than an hour and you'll be in my arms. Just say the word, Win. I mean it."

She stifled a giggle, and her eyes were wide. "Oh my gosh. Can we really do this?"

"I sort of have my hopes up that we can."

"Me, too. Just get here — quickly but carefully!"

"Will do," he chuckled, and she could hear the excitement in his voice.

He texted her when he made it Nags Head Beach. She gave him specific instructions to park at the beach near their property, and to follow the boardwalk which led to the oceanfront. Winnie stepped out her back door to meet him in the sand. She had turned off the outside cameras, so she felt completely at ease when she initiated a kiss that could have effortlessly gone on forever.

She was still in Baylor's arms when he spoke. "I don't want us to get caught out here. All I can think about is being with you. Take me inside."

Winnie reached for his hand and led him to the beach house. They stood together in the massive dimly lit living room that had cathedral ceilings and marble flooring. The entire back of the house was all windows. The blinds were still open on those windows and all Baylor could see was the dark night. It was risky and romantic at the same time and he wanted to take her right there on the floor. Instead, he watched her with her phone in her hands as she sent her husband a text. She told Milo that dinner was now in the fridge and she was going to bed. His response came a few minutes later.

Not hungry. Thanks anyway. Dealing with a crisis here.

Winnie read his text aloud to Baylor.

"Is that common for him?"

Winnie shook her head. "No. I wonder what's going on."

"You could ask him."

"I don't want to because, really, do I care? You and I are wasting precious time," she smiled at him in the way that she did when she wanted him and he practically unraveled.

Winnie instantly sent another text to Milo.

Okay. Good night.

An immediate response from Milo stated, *I love you, Wynette.* But Winnie never saw that message on the phone that was already placed face down on the table as she fell into Baylor's arms. A moment later, she led him by the hand to her bedroom.

"In here?" he asked, as they stepped through the doorway.

"Yes, in here, in my bed. I want to smell you on my pillow after you leave."

But neither one of them wanted to think about the moment when they would have to part ways again. For now, they only wanted to shut out the rest of the world.

Their mouths met. Their tongues tantalized each other. Winnie started tearing off her own clothes and Baylor reached for the button-fly on his denim. She pulled him by the hand over to her bed. She laid down and he was there with her. He pleasured her bare breasts with his hands, his mouth. Winnie arched her back and moaned his name. "I need you, Baylor."

"I love you so much, Win. I want to be with you forever."

"Show me," she enticed him, and he was more than willing to give her his full attention as he slowly kissed his way down her body. He found her folds, her core, and she dug her fingers into the sheets. There was never any other man for her. To touch her. To love her. She was lost in him and how he made her feel. The moment she released, Baylor straddled her, entered her, and thrusted himself inside her.

Winnie's hands gripped his ass as he repeatedly rocked over her. And she found another release just as Baylor let go of his.

Their time was precious and limited, but their love was endless. They came together again before Baylor had to leave in the middle of the night.

And in the morning Winnie inhaled a trace, an intoxicating scent, of him on her pillow.

Chapter 8

Adler was sitting in her highchair at the kitchen table. It was breakfast time when Milo walked in, wearing the same clothes as the day before. Winnie was still in her favorite short white terrycloth robe with her dark hair piled high in a topknot. Adler reacted to Milo's presence and once she had her moment with her daddy, Winnie spoke.

"You're just now getting home?"

He nodded as he rubbed the overnight stubble on this face with his hands. "Long night."

"Did you fix whatever problem you had?"

"Not yet."

"Were you working alone all night?"

"What the hell is that supposed to mean? Are you accusing me of having an affair?"

Winnie stepped back. *No. She was not. Why would she, after what she did with Baylor most of the previous night?* "No." She wanted to roll her eyes, given the fact that he had in fact cheated on her with one of the home health care nurses. "I'm only curious if you had help with whatever it is that you're dealing with."

"We were all there most of the night — my father and my uncles."

"Do you want to tell me what's going on?"

"No. I need to shower and get back there."

"Okay," was all she replied. And the funny thing was, Winnie could not have cared less what the Brands were dealing with at the bank. The only thing that mattered to her was her husband's absence last night had allowed her to be with Baylor.

Milo was livid. They had been smurfing their offshore accounts for decades, which involved small deposits of money over time into various accounts at multiple banks. Suspicion was never stirred that way, because when deposits are minimal no eyebrows are raised. Someone screwed up somewhere when 300 million dollars landed in one single account. And now that money was missing. Milo's father and his uncles had retraced their steps, rehashed them again, and then fretted and panicked all night long. They feared the only explanation was the FBI had been alerted and gotten involved. If that was the case, all of their lives were over. The Brands had been bankers in Nags Head Beach for generations. The boys running the show now could lose everything — including their freedom.

CONSEQUENCES

Milo was sick to his stomach. He fell into that business because his family owned it, and the thing about him was he loved it. Banking was in his blood. And when his father introduced him to a means to make millions of dollars, Milo didn't balk. He never had a keen sense of right from wrong anyway. He was all in, which meant if his father and uncles went down for drug trafficking — so would he.

He thought of Winnie and Adler. He was going to disappoint them in the worst way. He thought of Sally, his grandmother who was completely oblivious to the Brand's fortune being dirty money. He felt shame, but only because something had somehow gone wrong and the fear of being caught now overwhelmed him.

He took a steaming hot shower, shaved his face, got dressed in a tan suit, no tie, and went back into the kitchen. Adler was crawling at Winnie's feet as she loaded the dishwasher.

Winnie studied him for a long moment. Something was vastly off. He looked lost. His eyes were red and tired from a sleepless night, and his always-in-command attitude was gone. She had never seen him like this. Milo noticed that about his father last night too. The confident air was missing from his demeanor and he looked as if he had aged 10 years overnight. "Milo? Is everything alright? I mean, I know there's a crisis at the bank, but the way it's affecting you—"

"What?" he snapped at her. "Is that your way of telling me that I look bad? Or, are you actually showing some concern for your husband?"

Winnie shrugged. If he was going to be a dick about it, he didn't deserve her concern.

"I'm sorry," he said, looking down at the floor at Adler who was now pulling herself up on his leg. She fisted his pant leg and mustered the strength to stand upright for the first time as she teetered unsteadily on her little bare feet.

Milo's eyes met Winnie's, and for a moment they shared the mutual joy of witnessing their baby reach a milestone. Milo clapped heartily for her, and Winnie bent down to kiss those full cheeks on her face. "You pulled yourself up all by yourself! Mommy and daddy are so proud of you!" she cheered like the proudest mother on earth, and when she looked up at Milo from her knees down on the floor, she saw tears welling up in his eyes. She was always touched by his love for Adler. Little did she know that Milo was thinking how this could be one of the last happy moments for them to share as a family. Chances were great that he would miss some, or all, of his daughter's childhood if he was locked away in a prison cell.

"I think it might be time for me to mosey on," Remi spoke to her mother, using an expression her father had said for years. After breakfast, it was always time for him to *mosey on* to the bank. Remi and her father were closely bonded. He sweetly reminded her all the time that she was his special one, his little girl.

CONSEQUENCES

Sally didn't know what surprised her more — Remi already wanting to leave Nags Head Beach again, or hearing her say those words she had heard so many times throughout her marriage. Her husband had been gone for more than a decade, and there wasn't too much that she missed about him.

"Your father said that more times than I care to estimate," Sally scoffed.

"He did," Remi agreed. "Why did you stay with him, Mom?" This was the first time Remi had ever asked Sally that question. She thought it before, of course, and so had her brothers. It was evident under their roof that their parents' relationship was different. It was odd to watch, Remi concluded once she was old enough to understand relationships and love. The strange part of it all was that her father adored her mother — to a fault. The more he tried, the farther she recoiled. He was caring and loving to her one moment and unkind and hurtful the next. His apologies always fell on deaf ears and Sally eventually saw her husband as a man who had served his purpose in her life after she bore children. Over time, she was simply done with him.

"What kind of question is that?" Sally needed a stall tactic. This wasn't a discussion that she wanted to have with her daughter. The child she secretly conceived with her lover.

"I often wondered if you loved him."

"At one time, yes, I did. I used to tell myself to put a real effort into loving him as hard as I could, but I gave up on that eventually. Loving him was exhausting, to say the least. I always knew that I was the center of his universe, and his regard once made me feel like the brightest, most beautiful, desirable woman in the world. But, over time, I realized that I didn't love him half as much as I loved who he made me think I was."

"He worshiped you," Remi noted.

"I know he did, but he also suffocated me with his manic back and forth behavior," Sally admitted.

"Why haven't we ever talked about this before?"

"Because you never asked." Sally laughed out loud. "So, you feel it's time to move on again, huh? I'm curious how or what brings on that itch..."

"I can't really explain it other than I just feel it in my bones that it would be best." This time, Remi knew she didn't want to be around for the fallout of the Brands. It had been two weeks since she overheard Milo on the phone at the bank, and all was still quiet. She wondered if nothing would change, if that problem had been dealt with — or if there was a ticking time bomb about to blow their family to bits. The calm before the storm, as they say.

"I'll never understand the lure of it," Sally admitted, and she thought of Remington Boyd. She was angry with him for a long time for running, for being a man who would always need more. "I suppose the older I get, I see the importance of having the people you love around you. Loneliness can kill a person's spirit." She paused and stared at her daughter. She was a beauty. She turned the heads of both men and women. There were a handful of people on this earth who could effortlessly do that, and Remi always seemed oblivious to that gift.

CONSEQUENCES

"I'm not always alone, Mom. Meeting people is part of the draw for me. And, sometimes, in the least likely places I'll see a familiar face."

"Oh yeah? To me, that would be such a comfort — like a piece of home."

Remi nodded. "Last time that happened I was at a pub in Orange Beach, Alabama, and our old neighbor, Walt tapped me on the shoulder."

"Walt Seger?" Sally slapped her own knee. "Well, I'll be. He must be well into his 80s by now. I remember he moved away after Helen died, and I heard he was looking to settle down in a retirement community, but I never knew where he ended up."

"We sat down and had a beer and I thought it was going to be one of those conversations where we just talked about nothing at all, but he said something that I can't seem to erase from my brain. Words from a drunk old man shouldn't get under my skin, right?"

Sally sat up straighter. "I can't imagine Walt having any words of wisdom for a young woman."

"No. Just something to think about. In fact, those were the exact words he said to me as I walked away from him. Something to think about." Sally stayed silent as she watched her daughter stand up and walk over to the French doors which looked out to the backyard, to the rose garden. Remi stared out there for a long while before she turned back to her mother and spoke. "Tell me about the rose garden. Whatever gave you the idea to start one and nurture it, year after year?"

"The boys were all in school. Your dad worked day and night. I was in my early 40s and suddenly I had a keen focus on what mattered and what did not. I finally settled into myself and I no longer cared about the bullshit anymore. I knew who I was and what I wanted." Remi listened raptly as she had not ever heard her mother speak so personally about herself. She was always outspoken and direct, but she never had Remi's attention like this before. It was as if Remi, as silly as it seemed, finally saw her mother as a woman with genuine feelings and true desires. A woman who could separate herself from being a wife and a mother. "I didn't have to work, and volunteering just wasn't my thing. I wanted a rose garden. I hired a gardener to help me get started, to teach me all there was to know about nurturing one. After a year of his help, I was confident to carry on with it alone."

It appeared that Sally was done revealing the depths of her soul. Remi was miffed. If her mother taught her anything at all, it was to follow through. To speak your mind and seek what it is that you want. "Funny, Walt mentioned your gardener as well."

Sally forced herself to remain expressionless. "Really? He always was a nosy old fucker."

Remi stifled a laugh. "I think you're right about that. He said he remembered seeing the two of you together, working in the garden. I told him that I didn't remember a gardener during my childhood, and he seemed to get a real kick out of telling me that I had not been born yet. He called the gardener a drifter, and he told me that I was born after he left town."

"Oh for the love of God, what was the point of all his rambling!"

"I think you know," Remi stared at Sally.

"The hell I do! I told you, I hired a gardener for my newfound passion way back then, and would you just look at that rose garden decades later! It is still flourishing."

"Passion, huh? What was this gardener like, Mom? I mean, I already know he was a drifter. Like me, actually, as Walt said."

Sally scoffed. "What exactly did Walt imply?"

"Apparently there was an obvious chemistry between the two of you."

"I won't deny that," Sally answered, honestly.

"Just once, please talk to me as if I'm just another woman and not your daughter. What did that man mean to you?"

Sally knew that she owed Remi exactly what she was asking of her.

"For the first and only time in my life, I felt the dizzy-headed, heart-pounding, head-over-heels way that you're supposed to feel when you fall in love. It was the kind of at-first-sight love that feels so right that you just know you're with the person meant for you. It was only for a short while, but it was magical." There was a gleam in her mother's eyes as she spoke and clearly savored the memory of him.

"I don't even want to think about what this means," Remi stated as a matter of fact, "but it's not like I haven't already gone over and over it in my mind. I don't look like my brothers. I don't have the features of a Brand. Did you get pregnant by your lover,

Mother?"

Sally paused. *Jesus. This was not a conversation that she believed she would ever be forced to have with her daughter.* "He was a good man. I knew he couldn't stay. I could have bargained for a different ending, where no one left, but I didn't because I had a moral obligation to my family, my boys — and yes, my husband."

"How could you go back to Dad after experiencing that great love?"

"I told you, I chose my family. I had children to raise, and a baby on the way."

"Me…" Remi sighed. "I'm really not a Brand."

"Your father never knew that."

"Wait. Which one?" Remi snapped at her. "Your husband or your lover?"

"Both."

"So there's a man out there who never knew he had a child with you, because you never told him about me!"

Sally nodded.

"He's probably dead by now, just like my Dad — or, I mean, the man who I thought was my father."

"I don't know. I never tried to find him," Sally's voice trailed off.

"What was his name?"

CONSEQUENCES

After a short pause, Sally told her, "Remington Boyd."

Tears immediately sprung to Remi's eyes. "You've got to be kidding me!"

"I needed a part of him with me always, and you were that blessing for me."

"But you lied to me for my whole life!"

"I made a choice that I would freely make again if I had to do it all over."

"Of course you would," Remi's tone was snarky.

"A woman is a nurturer. It's a natural thing for us. But then there's this need for personal fulfilment. I overlooked that about myself for many years. I resented your father for the control he had over me and my life. I needed to feed my soul, and that's what my rose garden has done for me in more ways than one."

"I wish I didn't know the truth."

"Then leave it be."

"What if I tried to find him?"

"Then you would prove something I've always known, and that is, you are much more courageous than I am."

Remi halfheartedly smiled, and Sally reached for her hand.

Chapter 9

"So, the two of you are still able to sneak around?" Oakley eyed Winnie and Baylor as the three of them sat around the island in Baylor's kitchen. It was the first time in too long that they had all been together at the triplex. "How are you avoiding Milo's suspicion?"

Winnie felt like smiling. All was currently right in her world while she was there with those two. "Milo is consumed with work. Oddly enough, he doesn't even ask where I've been or what I'm doing." Winnie didn't elaborate that something had changed with him; that he was preoccupied and edgy all the time.

"Well we should be drinking to celebrate that!" Oakley stood up, ready to ransack Baylor's kitchen.

"Beer and wine in the fridge," Baylor told her, and Winnie wanted wine. It was barely noon, but no one objected. Oakley handed Baylor a longneck and then uncorked a bottle of Moscato for herself and Winnie, who she thought looked much healthier as she was beginning to put on weight again.

"So tell us what the latest is with your book…and Jack." Winnie added that Baylor told her she had been in Norfolk overnight for a few days.

"I do have some news," Oakley began, "but first I need to tell you guys that my birthfather showed up again. He was in line at one of my signings."

"I hope your security threw him out on his ass," Baylor spoke in no uncertain terms. He knew how much pain that man had caused Oakley.

"They would have if I hadn't wanted to speak to him in private."

"You did what?" Winnie placed her wine glass down after taking a generous sip of it.

"I know. Jack freaked out, too, but it was something I had to do. Although I don't know what I was expecting to hear. It was so strange being in the same room with him, hearing his voice. I didn't hold back. He knows how my whole life has teetered on this axis of mistrust and pain since the day he left me. He ended up getting defensive and blaming my mother for forcing him to leave."

"Even if that were true, he chose never to see you again and have an active role in your life," Winnie stated in disgust as she gulped more of her wine. It was going down really well.

"That's what I said."

"Have you talked to your mother about this?" Baylor inquired.

"Not yet. I need to do that in person, and I've been a little busy in Norfolk."

"Did you stay there to work on your book?" Winnie emptied her glass and placed it down on the granite surface in front of her.

"Look at you... let's get a refill on that!" Oakley giggled and again tipped the open bottle over Winnie's glass.

Baylor chuckled. "Slow down there, babe. You still have to drive and pick up a baby." Winnie giggled loudly, as she was already halfway to tipsy. She did have to make her way back to Nags Head Beach by late afternoon. Sally and Remi were watching Adler, because Remi was only spending a few more days in town and she wanted more time with the baby.

"Tell us about the book," Winnie redirected Oakley back to the subject at hand.

"I'm halfway finished with writing the sequel. Jack was happy with it, but he of course dove into it with his usual edits."

"Does that still bother you?" Baylor asked.

"Not as much, I guess. I mean, I get that it's his job."

CONSEQUENCES

"Are you two still dancing around the fact that you're in love and dying to tear off each other's clothes again?" Winnie giggled.

"The clothes have come off again," Oakley winked.

"Yay!" Winnie cheered, lifting her glass in the air and Baylor shook his head. *No more wine for that one.*

"Jack's commitment to me has never wavered. I could see the pain in his eyes that he felt for me when I confronted my father and pretty much walked away letdown and disappointed again. I don't know what I wanted to come of that brief reunion, but the fact is he hurt me and seeing him does not bring me peace. Jack has been my rock, so I finally stopped fighting what I want and that is to be with him. So, we spent a few days getting reacquainted."

Baylor chuckled, and Winnie was emotional. "I could not be happier for you."

"Oh honey," Oakley reached across the island for Winnie's hand, "thank you."

Time passed before Baylor suggested getting them something to eat, but the girls only wanted to drink. Finally, he served them both with tall glasses of iced water. "Time to wash the alcohol out of your bloodstreams, ladies."

They giggled some more.

Once they calmed down and began to sober up, Oakley attempted to escape.

"No, don't go. I still have at least one more hour before I have to hit the road," Winnie whined.

"I have errands to run, and I really should stop by my mother's house."

Winnie nodded. She understood.

"And besides, three becomes a crowd with us now."

"Don't think that, don't ever think that," Winnie reached for Oakley and pulled her into a close hug.

"Honestly, we had our time to catch up. Now you two hit the sheets before you run out of quality time to get naked."

They laughed before sharing a group hug. *This was friendship at its finest.*

Baylor turned to Winnie the moment Oakley was gone.

"You okay? Do you need more water?"

"I need you," she stepped closer to him and placed her palms on his broad chest.

"I'm serious, Win. You have to be coherent to drive back home."

"This is my home." She was emotional again.

"It is," he pulled her closer to him and held her, "and it always will be."

He held her hand and walked her up the stairway to his bedroom. They did need to take advantage of their precious little time.

Chapter 10

Oakley drove up to her parents' house and parked her car in the courtyard. Their home was massive and breathtakingly beautiful with large white pillars spanning the entire front of the structure, like something straight out of a fairytale. Oakley relished that kind of lavished lifestyle while she was growing up. She still enjoyed the perks of everything money could buy. And now success enabled her to earn her own fortune. She had more than enough money and she wouldn't deny that it mattered to her.

She rang the doorbell at her mother and stepfather's home in fear of arriving unannounced. When her mother swung open the door from the other side, Sondra Marks didn't look like she had a free moment to spare. She stood there in a little white tennis skirt, a powder blue sleeveless collared shirt and crisp, white tennis shoes. Her blonde hair, styled in a bob, had concealed gray roots which required a touch-up up every two weeks. She was in incredible shape for a woman in her late fifties as she swore by yoga and clean eating.

"Darling! Come in. I wish Trey was here to see you. He and I are so proud of your success. I mean, he has been boasting about you to everyone."

Oakley smiled "Trey has always been in my corner." He was a good man.

"He certainly is proud of you. We both are."

"I'm grateful that he's treated me as his own daughter all my life."

"And he kept your bank account replenished," her mother cackled. Her comment was tacky to Oakley. The two of them walked through the foyer and into the living room. Sondra sat down on the sofa, but Oakley chose to stand. She was too nervous to relax.

"Money matters to you mom, I get that. You taught me to feel the same." Oakley was too young to remember the years when her mother worked as a hairstylist at a salon in Edenton. She stood on her feet for 12 hours a day just to make ends meet. She was the sole bread winner for most of her first marriage, as Oakley's birthfather was always out of work.

"There's nothing wrong with living well. I believe that never lacking the funds to pay our bills in full and to always enjoy the finer things in life has brought us much happiness. Am I wrong?"

"No," Oakley agreed with her mother. "But I do wonder if there was ever a time in your life when you were just plain happy without all the luxuries."

CONSEQUENCES

"Do you mean when we lived in a state of panic and worry as there wasn't enough money every month to appease the bill collectors? I worked tirelessly, and I still came up short for our family."

"What about my father?"

"What about him? He never held a job for longer than six months. He stayed home with you while I did hair all day long."

"I do remember spending a lot of time with him." It pained Oakley to say those words because once he left, she never stopped missing him. There was such a void in her heart for a man she idolized as a very young child.

"I still regret not putting you in therapy all those years ago. It would have brought you some closure, I think. Here you are, 31 years old, and you're still letting it affect you."

"Nothing could have fixed how I felt. All I wanted was for him to come back."

"I know."

"How about you, mom? Before you met Trey and got married again, did you ever wish for him to come back to us?"

"No, because I knew that we could not continue to live so poorly."

"So it was about money for you? If my father had been rich, you would have been blissfully happy?"

"I didn't say that," Sondra admitted. "I loved that man, and he completed me for many years. Until love just wasn't enough anymore."

"He found me recently. Twice now, he has just shown up."

Her mother's facial expression was a cross between shocked and annoyed. "I assume he wanted money, knowing that you are rich and famous now."

"I've always been wealthy," Oakley bluntly stated.

"Is that why he showed up? He wanted money?"

Oakley shook her head. "No."

"Surely you didn't give him the time of day! He couldn't be more undeserving of your attention."

"I confronted him about leaving us." Oakley watched her mother's expression turn stone cold. "He said something that I'd like you to clarify for me. He said that you kicked him out of our home and out of our lives. Is that true, Mom?"

"He couldn't provide for us, and I grew sick and tired of carrying that burden alone."

"That's not what I asked you."

"I told him to leave and to stay out of your life if he couldn't be anything but a worthless provider."

But he wasn't a worthless father. He was attentive and loving and absolutely everything a little girl needed from her daddy.

"He loved me. How could you not have seen that?"

"He clearly didn't put up a fight, Oakley. I forced him to leave, but I really couldn't make him abandon his own child. That was on him." Which was what everyone had been restating. *Jack.*

CONSEQUENCES

Winnie. Baylor.

"So you just stopped loving him when he didn't provide for his family?"

"No." Sondra's voice was somber. "I just chose a better life, and quite frankly love has never had anything to do with it."

This should not have surprised Oakley, but to actually hear her mother say those words aloud was disheartening. She did realize, though, that it wasn't as if Trey Marks hadn't been looking for arm candy when he reciprocated her mother's not-so-subtle advances. Whatever their relationship, it was between them. Oakley had accepted that a long time ago.

"I'm in love for the first time in my life," it felt freeing for Oakley to say those words, "and I cannot imagine ever giving up Jack for anything — even if he and I both were dirt poor."

"Easier said than done, especially when you're not living it."

Perhaps her mother was right.

"Leave money and fortune out of this for a moment, please, Mom. Just tell me what your relationship was like for you and my Daddy. Will you do that for me?"

Her mother appeared emotional, then abruptly regained her composure. "He was charming and confident, loving and attentive. There was a time when he made promises that he kept, no matter what. But then he started drinking. He blamed me for his dependence on alcohol because I pressured him to get a job and to be a useful man — and he would say he just needed something to take the edge off. It got out of hand, Oakley. I didn't want you exposed to that, and I also wanted to save myself from going down that dark hole with him. I loved him. Don't ever think I didn't. I just loved myself, and my child, more."

Chapter 11

With a few suitcases packed in the back of her midsize SUV and a cooler for the road, Remi left Nags Head Beach once again. The goodbye she shared with Sally was different this time. Her mother, who always kept a stiff upper lip, fought tears. Her parting words were, "I hope you find what you're looking for. Go get some answers, honey." Sally had always been the type of mother who allowed Remi to make her own mistakes. This was off character coming from a woman who spoke her mind and knew no boundaries, but she had chosen to raise her daughter with confidence and grace. Remi held close to her heart the words that Sally spoke to her the first time she left home many years ago.

"I'm not a big believer in other people telling me what's good, what's bad, or what I should be doing. I make up my own mind. You've got to be accountable to yourself in this world. Own your life. Your failures should be because you made the choice, not anyone else deciding anything for you."

Remi had one final stop to make before she left North Carolina. She had been to Edenton many times through the years, but never to Orion Lane. Today, that was her destination for the sole purpose of doing the right thing.

Winnie stood on the pier alone. No one else was home at the triplex, and she had just put Adler down for a nap in her crib. She held the baby monitor in her hand now. There was a lot weighing on her mind and she thought it would be best to retreat to the place that brought her peace.

She and Milo had another serious argument the previous night, which was becoming a common occurrence with him in recent weeks. He suggested the three of them take a vacation, even out of the country, and Winnie objected. He was adamant about them making memories as a family, and he once again pressured her to let him move back into her bedroom. Winnie now kept her bedroom door locked at night, in fear of him coming to her.

"Nothing changes between us, because you will not meet me halfway!" he raised his voice at her.

"Don't pressure me," was all she had said in return.

Milo glared at her before he replied, "I have been more patient than you deserve." His words had become hurtful again. He was edgy and distant most of the time, and then almost instantly he would turnaround and expect her to want to spend quality time together as a family — and want him again. The thought of Milo touching her, and being intimate with him, repulsed her. Winnie needed to keep her emotions in check so she would not revert to binging and purging. She already was back to binging, and had been putting on more weight. She struggled to find a sense of calm at the beach house, so she returned with Adler to the waterfront. The trees at the far edge of the bay had begun to turn colors for fall even before the temperatures turned cooler.

CONSEQUENCES

Winnie glanced down at the video monitor in her hand. She was grateful for the alone time out there as Adler remained asleep. She nearly dropped the monitor, though, when she was startled by a voice off the pier. "I thought I'd find you out here."

It was Remi.

"What in the world?" Winnie was both taken aback and baffled to see her there. "How did you know I'd be here?" It would have been rude to ask, *and why are you here?*

"I took a chance. This is my last stop before I get the hell out of dodge for awhile." They both laughed and Winnie wondered if Remi realized how alike she and Sally were sometimes.

"I was hoping you could stay for awhile. Adler has gotten used to seeing you at Sally's."

A smiled stretched across Remi's face. "I enjoy her so much, and she truly was one of the reasons why I stayed for as long as I did."

"Adler is a lucky girl to have so many people in her life who care so much."

"She's easy to love. Really, I've never met a baby who was such a people magnet. She draws us in and, before we know it, we are in love with her little round face and those dark eyes."

Winnie smiled proudly. Having a child changed in her in many ways. Adler most definitely had a way of bringing people together. Winnie liked Remi, and she felt fortunate to have had this chance to meet her. For as long as she had known Sally, she only heard about her daughter, the one Brand child who did not live in Nags Head Beach. She was the world traveler. It was strange to think that she was Milo's aunt, yet they were only a few years apart in age.

"What brings you here, Remi?" Winnie's words were gentle, like if she had reached out and wrapped her arm around her as the two of them stood on the pier overlooking the bay.

It was awhile before Remi took her eyes off the water and answered her.

"I grew up watching my mother in a loveless marriage. I don't see that any of my brothers are truly happy with the relationships they're in. And then there's Milo. My mother says he is a Brand through and through the way he adores you and his baby, but it's to a fault, isn't it? I mean, there's a mutual admiration between them as father and daughter, but it's not the same with you, is it, Winnie?"

"Why is this important for you to discuss?" Winnie felt uncomfortable.

"The very last thing that I want to be is the person behind bringing down anyone in my family. I love my brothers and my nephew — and now I have a great niece. I just need to leave the town that is saturated with everything Brand. My family can be too much sometimes. More than even I realized." Winnie stayed quiet and listened. "I know that my mother passed me off as a Brand."

Winnie eyes widened. *Did Remi know that she also knew the truth?*

CONSEQUENCES

"It's okay. I'm aware that my mother confided in you, and only you, apparently."

So that's why she was leaving. "I can't imagine how you're feeling, Remi. If you're angry with Sally, please try to see where she was coming from. She found a love she had never known. You were a gift from that special time in her life. Maybe someday, once you've had time to process this, you will—"

"Understand?" Remi interrupted her. "I'm not angry with my mother, or terribly hurt that she kept the truth from me." Sally obviously had raised a remarkable daughter, and Winnie felt proud to know someone so selfless and forgiving. "To be honest, I've often felt like a square peg trying to fit into a round hole within my entire family. I guess subconsciously I knew that I wasn't one of them."

"Remi," Winnie spoke softly, "they all adore you. You must see and continue to believe that."

"I do," she smiled. "Nothing has changed. They are still my family. For now, I don't think anyone else needs to know the truth about this. It's between my mother and I, and perhaps I'll find some closure somewhere out there."

Remi's subtle implication instantly caught Winnie's attention. "You're going to search for him, aren't you?"

"I don't know if it's him that I'll actually find. He could be gone from this world already." *Just like the father who raised her.* "I do hope to find out his story; what his life was like, where he ended up. I don't even have a photograph to know what he looked like."

"I hope you find all the answers, I really do," this time Winnie reached for Remi and squeezed her hand.

"I didn't come here today to tell you that I know that you know," they both laughed. "I need to say this one more time, I love my brothers. I am in no way turning on my family." Winnie creased her brow and waited for Remi to clarify what she meant. "Something is going on at my family's bank. I overheard one end of a phone conversation. It was Milo, and he was really upset about an overseas transaction gone wrong. Winnie, no one else knows this. I don't want to burden my mother with something that might not even be factual. I just have a feeling that things are not on the up and up. My brothers and Milo could be in serious legal trouble."

And there it was. A piece of the puzzle that Winnie wasn't even searching for. But, in recent weeks, she had recognized the evident change in Milo. The questions that surfaced in her mind right now nearly overwhelmed her. She didn't even know where or how to begin.

"What did you overhear?"

"There's money missing in an offshore account. A lot of money. Three hundred million dollars. Milo was irate and making demands on the phone when I left his office before he knew I was there. I don't know anything more, Winnie. As I said, I've kept this to myself until now."

"Why are you telling me this?"

CONSEQUENCES

"Honestly, I struggled with that. I don't want to see the fallout of my family. I don't even know if that can happen still. The issue may not have been as big as I perceived."

"I don't know where to begin," but Winnie knew for certain that she wouldn't ignore this.

"Just don't confront Milo. That would be a huge mistake."

Winnie agreed. Remi was entirely more worldly than Winnie would ever be. She felt like grabbing her by the shoulders and begging her to for guidance. "What would you do if you were me?"

"Just sit back and watch how things play out, or you could involve the FBI. It would be a simple tip off, Winnie. That's all." Although Remi believed it was possible that the feds already were watching the Brands.

Winnie's thoughts raced. Her life as she knew it could end. She imagined this as a way out of her marriage, a means to an end and it would be because of Milo's own doing. There was a fighting chance for her now. A life with Baylor was no longer out of reach. She might not be trapped after all. And then there was Adler. Milo was her father, a loving and doting one from the day she was born. Winnie felt as if she was in the middle of a tug of war inside her mind right now.

"You don't have to do anything right at this moment. Take some time to process what I've told you. Be careful around Milo, but consider being a little more inquisitive about his work…or snoop on his laptop or go through his briefcase. I don't know, I feel like I'm talking out a scene from a movie. Just stay alert, Winnie."

She nodded. "I don't know what to say to you. Thank you seems insensitive. This is your family. And I love and respect Sally. Those are her sons and her grandson; she adores every last one of them."

"That's why I couldn't tell her," Remi stated.

"But she also has been in my corner all this time. Sally knows I'm stuck and being controlled by Milo with his so-called image of happily-ever-after."

"I know. It's okay to think it and to say it. Winnie, this could be your way out."

Chapter 12

By the time Milo graduated from high school, he already knew everything there was to know about becoming a banker. Still, his father insisted that he spend the next four years attending college to earn a business degree. He told him, precisely, to enjoy himself and to just get passing grades. He noted that he had the rest of his life to work hard; it was time to play; a secure job awaited him after. Milo abided by his father's wishes, and at 22 years old he began his career at Brand First National Bank.

Not long after he settled into his position, working alongside his father and uncles, Thomas introduced Milo to a whole new world within their banking operation. The Brands didn't just own and manage a bank in Nags Head Beach. Their grand fortune had not come from banking alone. Money laundering and drug trafficking went hand-in-hand for them; all of it was masterminded by the Brand men. They were submerged in the illegal black market of cultivation, manufacture, and the distribution and sale of drugs. Their corporate-style drug trafficking scheme stretched across the United States and overseas. They recruited and trained cash couriers who would pick up the drug money — often times stuffed into shopping bags, duffle bags, or shoeboxes — and then deposited it into several different banks. The funds had to be split into small increments, ranging from $22,000 to $44,000, before being deposited into funnel accounts that would eventually be wired to Brand First National. This illegal scheming had gone on for the last decade. Following the death of Thomas Brand, Sr., his heirs inherited the reign of the bank and augmented their family fortune.

Just weeks ago, something went wrong in the Netherlands when $300 million was mishandled. The drugs for cash exchange took place in a warehouse. There was a miscommunication between the cash couriers afterward. The bills had yet to be divided into those smaller increments before too much money was deposited at one bank. By the time the courier who errored was made aware of the mistake and ordered to retrieve the money back from the bank, all of it was missing. Milo, his father, and his uncles, had yet to locate those hundreds of millions of dollars. They were sure they were being watched.

CONSEQUENCES

Money laundering and drug trafficking cases were never exposed overnight. The feds were known to take their time to dot every 'i' and cross every 't.' It was just a matter of time though.

Milo closed the door behind him when he entered his father's executive office. This was the man who taught him everything about life. *How to go after what you want, and to never settle for anything less. How to treat a woman. To play hard, but work harder.*

His father's hair looked whiter, and the lines around his eyes had deepened. Milo had utmost respect for him, but as of late a part of him hated him for what he had brought into their company and into their lives. Sure, they had pulled off making millions of dollars that they never would have seen if they continued to be legit with their finances and investments. But, if they were caught, they could lose everything. It was gamble that none of them questioned, ever. The regret ran deep now.

"Milo, come in. Anything new?"

"No," he shook his head. "Everything remains at a standstill. We still haven't touched any of our accounts anywhere. No deposits, no wired funds."

"How long can that go on?" They were already losing money. "The feds will sit on this for as long as it takes." Thomas' impatience grew.

"Maybe, but why give them what they need any sooner than we have to?" Milo stood before his father's desk rocking on the heels of his dress shoes with his hands in pant pockets.

"Do you have a personal plan in place?"

"What can I do?" Milo all but shrugged. "If I flee, I leave behind my wife and child. I suggested we take an extended vacation, just the three of us, somewhere far, and secluded."

"And?"

"My wife refused."

"She sure does a lot of that. Have you claimed your place in her bed again?"

Milo stared back at his father. "Would I be bending my administrative assistant over my desk if I had my wife back in every sense of the word?"

His father chuckled. "A man's gotta do what I man's gotta do."

"This operation, this brainchild of yours," Milo changed the subject, "it worked for so long; for years." It sickened him to think they all were about to meet their downfall. And there wasn't a damn thing any of them could do to save themselves. "I'll point your question back at you and ask, do you have a plan in place, Dad?"

Milo watched his father roll back his burgundy leather chair just enough to open the top desk drawer. And then he gently placed a revolver on his desktop.

"You've got to be kidding me," Milo spun around on his heels and ran his hands through his hair, which left sticky product residue on his fingers. "That's your answer?"

CONSEQUENCES

"I won't let them lock me up," was all he said. And, suddenly, the man who Milo grew up watching, worshiping, and imitating, was nothing more to him than a coward.

Oakley's first novel had taken her an entire decade to write. It was the result of a lifelong inspiration and years of work researching, writing, and revising. Writing wasn't always easy for her as she had worked meticulously to come up with compelling characters, settings, details, and that indefinable "it" that makes a story work.

The moment her book was published, it became a huge success — which meant a second novel loomed. Most authors have a choice at that point to crank out something relatively quickly, or sit back with their royalty checks and take just as long on their second novel as their first. That decision was instantly made for Oakley. Harper Publishing wanted a sequel within several months. Oakley was feeling the weight of that demand rather strongly now. She enjoyed the fame and her public position. It was the pressure to write a second story to be as good or better than the first. She had moments of inspiration and lulls of writer's block. She wondered if she was a victim of her own success and something had tainted her creative impulse. When she attempted to explain this to Jack, he didn't believe for a second that Oakley was a writer who only had one book in her.

"You need to channel how inspired you were, a few months back, to write the rest of this story. You had a clear vision and a real fire in your soul to finish this." The two of them had just returned to his condo together after working all day. They were standing in his kitchen, debating on where they wanted to order take-out for dinner, when Oakley brought up how she contemplated deleting the entire chapter she had written just hours ago.

"I did, and I feel like I poured all of that into the first half of this book — but I'm tapped out. What if that's all I got?"

Jack stepped closer to her and cupped her face in both of his hands. "Doubting yourself under pressure is completely normal. The world is full of people who are struggling every day to write and publish one novel. The idea that you would have the opportunity to publish a second and now want to take a pass on it is unheard of."

"You're upset with me," Oakley noted, and she pulled away from him.

"Not at all. I just want to help you see that you've changed lives with your words. You've seen the sincere faces of your readers and heard them tell you firsthand that your book was relatable to them. You didn't create that work of art for the money or the fame. You wanted to send a message, and it was well received. No woman should ever put up with a man who degrades her and hurts her. There are victims out there, Oak, and many of them have picked up your book and read it, front to back. And now they are expecting more, as they are waiting with bated breath for you to write an ending that will give them hope. Don't let them, or yourself, down. Giving up will lead to regret."

"Is this a pep talk, Harper?" she smiled at him.

"You know it," he was relieved to see that he may have gotten through to her.

"How about if you stay with me for awhile. Spend your days writing in my office, or right here in this house. I'll be an arms-length away if you need a confidence boost or a hard-ass editor."

"I didn't bring enough clothes with me for an extended stay."

He saw that look in her eyes. "Who needs clothing…?" Jack closed the space between them and kissed her full on the mouth.

With her lips still on his, Oakley spoke as she grabbed for his rear, "I'd like to focus on your hard ass now."

Chapter 13

Winnie watched Milo closely as he sat on their living room sofa with a laptop on his legs. He wasn't focused on his child who was playing at his feet, or his wife who just mentioned how delicious their dinner was after he surprised her with takeout from her favorite seafood restaurant.

"Thanks again, Milo," she repeated.

"What?" he looked up when he heard his name.

"Dinner. It was so good."

"Right, yeah. I wanted to do something nice for you."

Why? She thought. *What did he want in return?*

CONSEQUENCES

"What are you working on so intently over there?" Winnie never cared to ask him about anything related to the bank before. She hoped that inquisition wasn't too obvious.

"Boring bank stuff to anyone else who doesn't love it like I do," he chuckled to himself, and Winnie wondered if that was his cover, or if she was reading into something that wasn't there. *Maybe Remi had overreacted?*

"Have you always wanted to be a part of the family business, or was it just expected of you?"

"Both, actually," he noted, and his eyes were back on the screen on his lap.

"Do you think you will encourage Adler to be a part of it one day?"

"Absolutely not," Milo was quick to answer. "It's no place for her."

Winnie took offense to that as a woman. "What do you mean? Because she's not a male? Is that why Remi and your sisters are not a part of it? Is there some kind of testosterone requirement?"

Milo rolled his eyes. "Of course not. None of them have ever shown any interest in banking, that's all."

"Then, if Adler wants to follow in your footsteps, you wouldn't steer her away?"

"I said it's no place for her." There was adamancy in his voice. Winnie clearly had touched a nerve. "I don't want her to work for me or with me or share that kind of stressful setting with me every day of her adult life. I want her to always be able to separate her father from the banker." Milo implied that he wasn't the same person at home versus at work.

"You do seem stressed most days," she stated as a matter of fact.

Lately, yes. "More often than not."

"Do you ever wish you could get out of it and away from being under your father's thumb?" Winnie may have gone too far with that question.

Milo looked at her for a long moment before he answered. "It's obvious that you don't like my father very much. I don't see my career as being under my father's control in any way. I am my own man. I make independent business decisions. He showed me the ropes many years ago and then set me free." He thought of all he was taught by the man he respected and admired — and the danger and the trouble that unraveled because of him.

"I just see Brand First National as Adler's legacy and I guess I don't understand why you don't." She was playing him. That statement could not have been farther from the truth. Winnie saw how ruthless both Thomas Brand and his son could be. Why would she want her daughter anywhere near that? She wanted Adler to grow with the same values and beliefs as she did. Money and power certainly weren't everything. Her life with Milo proved it.

"Since when do you care about something like that? If I didn't know any better, I'd believe you were beginning to accept being a Brand." He smiled, and she shook her head at him. *Never.*

CONSEQUENCES

When Winnie didn't verbally respond, he spoke again, and then it was clear to her that something dire was going on. "I never want to let you or my daughter down. Don't ever lose sight of that. You are both my world. I could give up and live without everything else, but the two of you."

"Is there something you're not telling me? You appear to be distracted or worried all the time, and now you make it sound as if something could change." That was a bold move for Winnie, and the fact that she could feel her heartrate quicken told her that she was entirely out of her comfort zone with him. Most times she didn't ask questions, nor cared to pry. He did his thing, and she did hers. Yet she was trapped in this life with him because that's how Milo Brand rolled. Winnie couldn't deny that she was nervous about Remi's warning and what could be pending, but at the same time she had a renewed spark of hope that had been nonexistent for far too long.

"Something could change," Milo repeated her words. "I can't get into it, because it complicated. Let's just tuck Adler into bed and call it a night."

"I'm here if you want to talk about it, Milo. I am your wife."

"Maybe I need to be reminded that I have your trust and your loyalty." Winnie was suddenly panicked that she had gone too far.

Chapter 14

Winnie could not sleep soundly. She was uncomfortable with how she felt about Milo. He touched her tonight. Together, they tucked their baby into her crib, and then in the hallway outside of her nursery, Milo pulled Winnie too close for comfort. He kissed her open-mouthed and pushed his groin up against her middle. She instantly pulled away from him, but not before he grazed her nipple through her t-shirt. His touch repulsed her, and she had not kissed him back. She rejected him once again and left him standing in the hallway alone. He was frustrated and angry, and completely out of patience. Keeping him out of her bed was becoming more difficult. His aggressive advances frightened Winnie tonight, and she was scared out of her mind when she heard him turn the doorknob to her locked bedroom door after she had taken a shower and gotten into bed. He never spoke to her from the other side of the door, but Winnie knew he was there for awhile before he left and returned to the guest bedroom where he slept on the opposite end of the house.

CONSEQUENCES

Somehow she was finally able to relax and had drifted off to sleep hours later. She was dreaming that an alarm was sounding, but she couldn't place where she was or pinpoint the loud noise. Suddenly, Winnie was jolted awake. She sat straight up in her bed just as her bedroom door was kicked in. She opened her mouth to react, but nothing came out. Two men in all black wearing caps on their heads with bold capital letters across the front were in her bedroom and pointing guns at her.

"FBI! Are you Wynette Brand?" One of them spoke loudly to be heard over the same noise she heard in her sleep. It was their house alarm system reacting to the break in.

"Yes!" She shielded herself with the blankets on the bed. "What the hell is going on here?" She was trembling so badly that her voiced quaked. Their guns were no longer drawn. At that moment, Winnie jumped out of bed. One of the federal agents stepped forward to stop her, to block her way. "I have a baby in this house, just across the hall!"

"We are not here for you or your baby. Tell us where your husband is."

Winnie's eyes widened. "The bedroom in the opposite wing," she freely told them. If she was supposed to lie, or attempt to buy enough time for him to run — she didn't. All she cared about was getting to her child.

Several minutes later, Winnie held a whimpering Adler in her arms as she scrambled to disable the alarm system. And just like that, there was silence. She could have heard a pin drop in that mansion on the beach when she turned to see Milo, handcuffed, with a half a dozen federal agents near him.

There were jumbled words, or maybe the voices had only sounded incomprehensible to her because her heart was pounding in her ears. But then, what she heard was suddenly clear. Milo was being arrested and charged with money laundering and drug trafficking. Brand First National Bank was under investigation for 11 counts of criminal activity. They were taking Milo into federal custody. This was a joint FBI and IRS investigation. Milo had a right to an attorney, but for now he was advised to remain silent.

Winnie held Adler tightly in her arms. She was relaxed and had closed her eyes again. Winnie kept her distance from Milo. She watched him hang his head and then lift it to catch her eye. She thought she saw shame or embarrassment, but she wasn't exactly sure. He certainly was not as shocked as she felt. The federal agents began to move him through the house. "Wait for me…" she heard Milo speak out to her as they closed the front door of their beach house behind them. Just like that, everyone was gone, merely minutes after their home had been invaded in the middle of the night and a human being was seized. And it was unclear to Winnie if he was ever coming back, because Milo Brand wasn't a free man anymore. He was a detained criminal.

It was two o'clock in the morning when Baylor's ringtone startled him. He sat up and fumbled to reach for his phone, which was charging on the nightstand beside his bed. The moment he opened his eyes just enough to focus on the caller ID, he ripped out the charge cord and answered the call. "Winnie?"

"Baylor," her voice was still shaky. "I didn't know who else to call." Her thoughts had raced after Milo was gone. Should she contact his father? His brothers? Contemplating that was almost comical as Winnie believed they too were guilty of everything Milo had done. There was no way he worked alone. Milo descended from a legacy of powerful, arrogant men.

"Tell me what's going on…"

"Could you just get here as soon as you can?"

There was a short pause on the Baylor's end. "Is Milo there with you?"

"No. He's gone."

Baylor had absolutely no idea what *gone* meant. And at this point, he didn't even care. Suddenly all he was concerned about was getting to her, and making sure that Winnie and AJ were safe and unharmed because something obviously had changed.

"I'm on my way."

Chapter 15

"So you knew something was going to happen?" Baylor asked Winnie, once she explained everything, starting with Remi confiding in her as well as Milo's edgy behavior, which led to his vague admission that something could change.

"I had no idea that they would literally hunt him down in the middle of the night." They sat on the sofa together in Winnie's living room. She laid Adler back down in her crib almost an hour ago and she was fast asleep again as if nothing happened. Winnie wished she too could so easily forget the events that just transpired.

CONSEQUENCES

"You should have told me sooner; the moment Remi came to you."

"It would not have mattered. It's not like I was able to fully confront Milo. I mean, he never confessed anything to me. I honestly had no idea what was going on or if anything would come of Remi's accidental eavesdropping. I mean, come on, drug trafficking and money laundering?"

Baylor couldn't ignore that this was a huge break for them. If Milo was convicted, and there was little doubt that he would be given that the FBI and IRS had been watching him for however long, that would be the end of Winnie's marriage. Her life with that egotistical son of a bitch would finally be over.

"You do know what this means," he began, and Winnie could see that spark in his eyes. "He's going down. All we have to do is sit back and watch it all end for him. And then his ending will be our new beginning."

Winnie reached for his hand. "I've felt that same hope, but I'm still completely shellshocked. He's Adler's father, and there's this possibility looming over my head that just like that I am going to be a single mother."

"You know that I want to be a family with the two of you."

"I want that, too," she told him, but she also could not ignore the bond between her baby girl and her father. Would she be faced with the choice to completely cut Milo out of Adler's life? She was getting ahead of herself and perhaps feeling caught up in Baylor's wishful thinking. The truth was, neither one of them knew if the Brands would indeed be held accountable for their crimes.

"I don't think you should stay here. Pack your bags and come back to the triplex for awhile. A.J. will love it." Winnie feared that Baylor was acting on impulse.

"I think I need to at least wait to hear from Milo." His words, as the agents escorted him away in handcuffs, stayed with her. *Wait for me.*

"I don't see him being allowed to post bail and come home so soon, and besides, it doesn't feel safe here anymore. What if the feds come back to search or seize things in this house? I think it's safer if you get out of here."

All of that had already crossed her mind. Even still, Winnie believed picking up and leaving this second was premature. Yes, of course, she wanted to move back to the triplex, and she hoped with all her heart for that to happen for her and Adler. "I hear everything you're saying," Winnie spoke gently, "but I need a little time to see how this plays out. We don't know anything yet, and I have to get to Sally this morning before she hears this from anyone else."

Winnie used her key to let herself in the back door. It was after eight o'clock in the morning so she knew Sally would be awake. She expected to find her sitting at the kitchen table, sipping a cup of black coffee. Instead, she was holding her coffee mug and standing directly in front of the living room TV. A local news channel reported the story. Winnie stood back to watch and listen as well, as the coverage continued.

CONSEQUENCES

The four Brands were arrested by FBI agents in their separate homes shortly after midnight. Three brothers and one second generation male, all own and operate Brand First National Bank in Nags Head Beach. They were charged with 11 counts related to drug trafficking and money laundering. This illegal activity was said to include unregulated financial systems across the country and overseas. All four men currently are being detained at an FBI detention center.

This was new information for Winnie. She had not heard from Milo or anyone else. She assumed he was not permitted to make any phone calls, other than to contact a lawyer. This was surreal to comprehend — for both Winnie and for Sally.

Sally turned to face Winnie once the news segment concluded. She stood there in her sleeveless white nightgown and fuzzy gray house slippers, and she looked as if her spirit had been crushed. "Well, I'll be. Those are my boys, and my grandson. How do I hold my head up high now? This should surprise me, and it does in some way, but I also find their greed and their inability to shun risky behavior so typical of them. Every last one of them. But, where does that leave the bank now? And our family?"

"And you, as well, Sally," Winnie stated, sincerely. "All of our lives are going to change."

Sally pursed her lips to blow her hot coffee before taking a cautious sip. "That's all of my children, except for my girl. I suppose there's no need to tell you again why she's good and moral. Those boys are rotten to their core, and I blame them for Milo's downfall. He was a good boy with a caring heart until he grew up and waltzed through those bank doors." Winnie saw those glimpses of good in Milo. She prayed that Adler didn't inherit any of the Brand genes which could tempt her to explore a path of wrongdoing in her life.

"I don't know what to say. I didn't see any of this coming with Milo; I guess because I never cared to pay attention or thought twice about where all the money was coming from. For as little as I knew, I bought into the fact that the banking business was profitable well into the millions."

"When my husband was alive and working his tail off at that bank, there was good money coming in, but nothing like over the last decade. Am I to assume that my grown sons got their hands dirty after their father died?"

"Seems that way," Winnie replied, "but I don't know. I would assume a lot of information will come out once their case goes to court."

"I don't have the slightest idea how many years of their freedom will be taken away."

"Drugs and money laundering are serious crimes," Winnie noted, "but people do walk away with very little consequences sometimes."

Sally eyed her closely. "I'm sure you want Milo to be punished and locked away for a long time."

Winnie stared back at her. "He's Adler's father. He's good for her, and she needs him just as much. How can I wish for him to miss out on seeing her grow up? I'm torn, though, because he hasn't been good to me. Before the FBI broke into our home last night, I had my bedroom door locked because I feared that my own husband was going to rape me. I cannot live like that for the rest of my life."

She solemnly shook her head. "Your side of the story always pisses me off," Sally stated as a matter of fact. "Yes, he is my grandson —my pride and joy at one time— but I can't ignore that he and his father and his uncles do deserve whatever is coming to them. Clearly, they all believed they were above the law and never expected to face any consequences."

"I'm sorry they've all hurt you like this," Winnie stepped closer to her and touched her bare arm.

"Me too, honey." Tears spilled over her eyes now. "I may be an old woman, and God knows I've harbored my share of mistakes, but I've always kept my chin up and carried on. I'm not as confident that I can do so anymore. The mere thought of my boys being locked up feels like it will be the death of me."

Chapter 16

"Unbelievable!" Oakley read the breaking news story on her phone. Winnie alerted her to what happened, and now Oakley could not stop thinking about it. She had been spending her time at Jack's condo, where she declared to stay until she completed writing the sequel.

"Goes to show you that we really don't know people at all, friends included." Jack referred to the friendship he and Milo had since college.

"I can't say that about my friends." She was one of the fortunate ones. "But, I do have to ask you how well you knew Milo? I mean, were you guys just buddies who talked about nothing at all or did you confide in each other about your lives?"

"Oak, a man who's chin deep in drug trafficking and money laundering hardly has time to call up his frat brother to bare his soul."

Oakley laughed.

"But, seriously, once Milo was illegally involved in all of that, he knew better than to confide in anyone. It's a bad deal all around. I'm sure his father sucked him into all things unethical, and I'll bet there's a high from it like no other when things are going good — but then there is such a thing as getting caught and facing the ramifications. No one ever goes there in their mind."

"I believe that, too, because there was a time that Winnie did see the good in Milo. It was short-lived, but she never would have married him if she knew half of what she knows now. He's a narcissist, Jack. He's awful to his wife."

"Why am I first hearing this from you now?"

"Milo was your friend. I respect friendships more than anything else in my life. I also keep so much of what Baylor and Winnie and I share private. It just goes without saying that we should protect and nourish it."

"I can respect that," Jack stated. "So, will Winnie stand by Milo through this? I can't imagine she would since he's been so cruel to her all this time."

"You have no idea — but I sure as hell hope not. She now has a way out of her miserable marriage. She has to run. And, besides, she has Baylor waiting for her. They will have a beautiful life together with Adler."

"What? Your Baylor? I thought you all were close like siblings or something?"

"Winnie has always loved Baylor. He was too little too late getting around to realizing that he reciprocated those feelings for her, so she got pregnant by another man and married him."

"Should you be telling me this? I thought you all kept everything in a vault?" Jack smirked.

"Right, but it looks like life is finally working in their favor and they no longer will have to resort to sex on the side."

Jack's eyes widened. "Winnie cheated on Milo?"

"Oh please, don't go there. Milo screwed his home health nurse while Winnie was under the same roof, in fact, she saw them through a cracked door."

Jack shook his head.

"What? I didn't think you were the type to judge."

"I'm not. I personally couldn't care less who is sleeping with who. I wasn't always pure and innocent." Oakley laughed out loud. *Neither was she.* "Maybe it's just me, but I look around and I see people throwing love away. Doesn't anybody ever stay together anymore?"

Oakley smiled at him, "Didn't someone write a song like that?"

"If they haven't, they should," he smiled back at her and the emotion met his eyes. Her heart was full, hearing those words from him. He could see how his words touched her. Jack pulled her to her feet and reeled her into his arms. He kissed her tenderly on the mouth, and once again she lost all control.

"I'm happy, Jack. Happier than I've ever been in my entire life. You're it for me. Always." She kissed him this time.

"Good. Because I don't ever want you to turn your back and run for cover."

She laughed. "I'm going to run upstairs and get under the covers."

Jack stifled a chuckle and took her in his arms again.

By the time they made their way to the bedroom, the stairway was littered with most of their clothing. Oakley was on the bed first, wearing only a pair of black leggings. She lost her shoes, shirt, and bra along the way. Jack wore a pair of jeans and nothing else. Before he joined her on the bed, he peeled those leggings off her body and dropped his jeans. Oakley pulled him by the elastic of his boxers and his manhood sprung upward. He kicked off those boxers and rolled her panties off her bottom and all the way down her legs. He kissed her ankle and then worked his way up. Her calf muscle had the definition of a runner. He always told her she had great legs... and rear... and chest. Beautiful face and all, her body was flawless. He took his time kissing her inner thigh, and she was about to lose her mind. Her body tensed and she arched her back. "You are pushing me to the brink of insanity!" He chuckled and moved to where his lady wanted him. Her core throbbed and he enticed her, again and again, until her whimpers and moans intensified with her final release. This woman, lying in his arms, turned him on like no other lover he had before her. Oakley touched his manhood and brought him into her mouth. What she could do to him was intoxicating. With complete abandon, Oakley pleasured him until he got close, and then Jack told her that he needed to be inside her. She laid back and parted her legs for him, as he eagerly made his way inside. He purposely took her, slowly, inch by inch, before she finally begged him. "Now, please." Their union was so intense that they could taste each other's perspiration. This was mad, passionate love making between two people who were made for each other, body and soul.

Chapter 17

It all came to light, just like Remi feared it would. By the time Sally called her, she already saw those Brand faces on the national news. Her brothers and her nephew were in unbelievably serious trouble now. Remi refrained from revealing that she had intercepted a warning and knew that the storm was coming. Her mother never before sounded so broken, and it angered Remi to know that the mindless, insensitive males in their family were to blame.

She was in Utah, staying at a remote ranch on more than 80 acres of land in the peaceful Indianola Valley. The main farmhouse was more than 5,000 square feet with five bedrooms. Remi chose the one-bedroom guest house on the grounds, which she thought was a mirror image of an old pioneer home — wood stove and all. So far, she had not noticed any activity at the main house, and she liked having the ranch all to herself. She walked the grounds at least twice a day. This place, in Fairview, Utah, had been her destination when she left Nags Head Beach. Rarely had Remi ever set out to end up in one particular place. This time, however, an online search had led her there. She was told that Remington Boyd wasn't one to settle down, but apparently at some point in his life he had. The only address connected to his name online was the ranch in Indianola Valley. And now Remi was there looking for answers.

Remi felt strangely comfortable there. She tried not to read too much into it, as she was still absorbing the truth that she had a father other than Thomas Brand, Sr. Still, she yearned to fill in the blanks, to solve this puzzle — because that man was a part of her history. She wanted to find out what happened to him after he left her mother behind in Nags Head Beach. In particular, what was his connection to that ranch?

When Remi contacted the owner about renting the guesthouse on the ranch grounds, she kept quiet the reason why she had chosen to stay there. Sooner or later, though, she would mention his name in Fairview, Utah. Someone had to know something about Remington Boyd — if he did indeed have roots there.

CONSEQUENCES

Remi went for another walk on the grounds. Each time, she set out to explore new areas. She had been past the grazing livestock, where she spotted cattle and sheep. The elevation at 6,000 feet allowed for warm days reaching 80 degrees and chilly nights in the 40s. The weather and the scenery out there was beautiful. Remi fought the fact that she easily felt at home there. It wasn't an admission she ever made; even Nags Head Beach was not somewhere she wanted to permanently call her home. She got closer to the main house this time. Since no one was renting it, as far as she knew, Remi wanted to take a look. There was a traditional swing, made of two ropes and a board seat, extended from a gigantic maple tree. Remi walked over there and didn't hesitate to sit down on the swing and grab ahold of those braided, polypropylene ropes. It was flexible, yet not too slippery to hold onto firmly. Remi lifted her feet off the ground and started to pump her legs. She tilted back and closed her eyes when the wind hit her face and blew through her long blonde hair. Swinging instantly symbolized how she felt out there on that ranch. *Free.*

The swing eventually slowed, and Remi scuffed the soles of her shoes on the ground, which was a patch of worn grass where many feet before her had landed to stop that swing in motion. She sat there for a long while before something caught her eye.

Roses. In a garden. Grouped by color.

She left the swing, still in motion behind her, when she walked through the grass.

Remi used to read about roses, and then she would ask her mother so many questions about the flower with the most beautiful form and exotic fragrance. The roses there were grown in a garden all their own. This bed was laid out in a geometric pattern, with tree roses at each corner and an arbor of climbing roses in the center. That focal point, like the center piece on a tabletop, forced Remi to step closer. Only yellow roses grew on that arbor. Persian yellow roses. It was the same layout, down to the colors. There were only red and yellow roses in this garden on the ranch; a carbon copy of Sally's garden in Nags Head Beach.

Roses were a special flower; loved by people all over the world, Sally used to tell Remi when she was a little girl. It was the one flower that didn't like competition from other plants. Had it been a coincidence that the man they called a drifter was skilled at creating and nurturing gardens for the flower that didn't want to share its space. Just like him. Was this rose garden also the work of Remington Boyd? Did his hands touch that soil?

Remi wanted to call Sally. She wanted to tell her where she was and what she found. *Drop everything. Just get here. You've got to see this.*

Not yet. Not until she was certain.

CONSEQUENCES

After hours spent alone in that rose garden, Remi returned to the guest house. There was a cherry-red high-back wooden rocking chair on the narrow front porch, which was where she was seated when she saw a vehicle driving on the lane road. She wondered if her peace and quiet streak had ended and if there were guests arriving to rent the main house. A moment later, she watched the vehicle veer away from the direction of the house and toward her place.

Remi waved the moment she realized it was the woman who rented the house to her. She had been the only person on the ranch the day that Remi arrived. Nina had given Remi a warm welcome. She liked her and realized she was happy to see her right now.

Nina stepped out of her car. She was tall, like Remi, with brown hair that was pulled back in a low ponytail. She looked like a rancher in her jeans and boots, but she was clearly very feminine too. Her fitted white t-shirt flattered her curves. Remi guessed she was in her thirties.

"Just checking on my tenant," Nina smiled. "How's it going out here all by your lonesome?" She approached the front porch and stood two steps below it.

"Wonderful. You've been very accommodating, thank you." The refrigerator and all the cabinets were well-stocked when she arrived. A grocery run wasn't even necessary yet.

"You're welcome. We're always happy to have guests here."

"So is the main house booked for anytime soon?" Remi didn't have immediate plans to leave.

"This weekend it is, but you can stay here for as long as you wish. The guest house isn't rented as often, so it's all yours."

"I guess most people don't travel alone," Remi noted, aloud. She certainly had, and clearly preferred it that way.

"Right," Nina agreed. "Do you? Always travel solo, I mean?"

"I do," Remi answered, suddenly contemplating if she should elaborate on what brought her to Indianola Valley. "Most of my travels are just the open road and me; wherever I end up is where I stay for awhile."

"How adventurous!" Nina was intrigued. "There's something to be said for that. I would love to hear your stories sometime, you know, so I could live vicariously through you — since I've never left Fairview." Remi laughed, but if she really thought about that, she cringed. She could not imagine never leaving home. *Come to find out, she had inherited that characteristic.*

Remi noticed Nina staring for a moment. "You look like you want to ask me something, but you're refraining."

Nina laughed. "Are you always so direct with people?"

"Forgive me, it's a quality that my mother passed on to me."

"I actually was wondering something, but I didn't want to pry."

"Ask away. If I don't want to answer you, I won't."

Nina laughed again. "I was only hoping your life of travel didn't mean that you are running from something."

"I don't see it that way. More like, I never felt like I belonged anywhere. It could be that I'm still looking for that. This time, though, my trip here was a predetermined destination."

"Why?"

"I traced someone's background online and I found that he once spent some time here, possibly years."

"Really? Share his name with me; I have two generations of relatives in Indianola Valley who could maybe help you."

That's what Remi was hoping for.

"Remington Boyd," It still felt strange for her to say his name out loud. "He spent some time in Nags Head Beach, working for my mother. He was her gardener." She didn't say that he was involved with her mother, nor that the rose garden behind the main house at the ranch was an exact replica of hers back home.

Nina's facial expression changed, but Remi wasn't quite sure how to read her initial reaction.

Chapter 18

One week after Milo's arrest, he called Winnie. She hesitated. There were so many unanswered questions, yet she still didn't want to talk to him.

"Hello, Milo."

"Winnie, it's good to hear your voice." She couldn't return the sentiment. And he simply overlooked her silence. "Listen, bond was set and paid. I need you to pick me up."

"Who paid for it?"

"Dad arranged for Mom to bail all of us out."

"You're talking hundreds of thousands of dollars, aren't you?"

CONSEQUENCES

"Yes, $250,000 for each of us."

Winnie realized that kind of money was within reach for them, unlike for most people. The Brands, however, were far from typical people — even before they were dubbed criminals.

"So what happens next?" She wasn't a legal expert, but everyone knew about court hearings, guilty or innocent verdicts, and sentencings. Sometimes legal cases took years to conclude. *Was this really her life now?*

"I'll return to my home. Come get me within the hour. I'm at the US Tacts Tracking Station."

"Where is that located?"

"In the federal courthouse. See you soon. Oh, and Winnie, bring Adler! I've missed her so much." He hung up the phone.

Winnie informed Baylor of what was going on. She had very little information to share, because Milo hadn't told her much of anything. Winnie only wanted to forewarn Baylor so he would not stop by the beach house, as he had every day or night since Milo's arrest.

She drove up to the courthouse and was prepared to get Adler out of the backseat to go inside. Before she had the chance, Milo came walking out of the building as if he just casted his vote in the national election. Proud and confident.

He reached the passenger door of her Jeep and got in. He turned around and fussed over Adler. It was heartwarming to see how excited she was to have her daddy back. Winnie, however, was far from pleased about her husband's return.

They shared meaningless small talk on the drive home. What they needed to discuss was probably best not to take place in a moving vehicle with a baby on board.

It was at least an hour later once Winnie confronted him and demanded answers. The moment Adler went down for a nap, Milo rushed into his office. This time, Winnie noticed he had not bothered to close the door. There was nothing to hide anymore, she assumed; his crimes were exposed. She walked through the doorway and interrupted as he hurriedly punched the keys on the laptop in front of him.

"What's so important?" she asked him.

"Work. We still have a bank to run."

"The news mentioned over thirty percent of the customers had already transferred their accounts out of there."

He shrugged and kept working.

"Don't you think I deserve to know what's happening now? I mean, how do you think I felt when our house was invaded in the middle of the night by armed agents — all because of your criminal activity?"

"You're disappointed and angry; that's completely understandable."

CONSEQUENCES

"How are you, your father, and your uncles going to avoid prison?"

"Well my father already made it clear that he will take his own life before he allows them to lock him up."

Winnie's eyes widened. "And no one is going to try and stop him?"

"It's his prerogative."

"What about you, Milo? I don't see how you cannot be scared out of your mind."

"I keep telling myself that it could be months before a court date is set, and I'm free until then. Meanwhile, I am paying my attorney to work feverishly to get me a lesser charge."

"What could happen? Is anyone telling you anything?"

Milo finally looked at her. "Penalties vary for both money laundering and drug trafficking, but there typically are fines, possessions and money seized, and I'm looking at 20 years."

"Oh my," Winnie covered her mouth with her hand. She was surprised, but not upset. More than anything, she hoped it was true. His imprisonment would be her freedom.

"It's sickening, I know," he stated, and she watched his demeanor soften. "I'm sorry, Wynette. Someday this will disappoint our daughter, too. You know that's the last thing I ever wanted."

"Then why did you continue to do it? Why even allow yourself to get sucked into something so dangerous and risky? You've gambled your entire life away. Adler will be an adult in 20 years..." and like hell if she was going to wait around for him like some sort of ridiculously loyal and submissive wife.

"I didn't have a choice, or at least that's the approach my attorney will take. The second-generation Brand did as he was told."

"Will something like that even work?"

"It's my life we're talking about, our life together as a family, so I will try anything to get less time. You have to understand that."

"What I understand is people like you have caused their families to lose everything."

"You and Adler will be well taken care of. There's money for you to live very comfortably."

"Dirty money?" she called him out because, dammit, she was embarrassed and angry.

"There's no use in acting all high and mighty. I do expect you to stay with me. This is our home and I want you to raise our daughter here. I want personal contact, as many visits that are allowed, with the two of you. But if you choose to cut me off, I will disown you both."

His tone and his body language seemed as if he was making some sort of business deal with her. All Winnie gathered from it was — Milo had lost his power. He could no longer use their daughter as leverage. He didn't have the ability to take her away from him and gain full custody, not if he was behind bars. *So he threatened to disown is child? What a worthless human being.*

She turned around so Milo would not see the overwhelming relief and the joy that she couldn't conceal. She silently questioned if he knew her at all? She lost her parents when she was in college. A horrific car accident left her with nothing but their debt. She learned how to be thrifty and resourceful, but she had been content living a low maintenance life. She had a steady job and the perfect home at the triplex on Orion Lane. And now she ached to live that kind of life again. Winnie closed his office door behind her. And that, to her, reflected how much she truly wanted to leave him in her past and begin again. If only the justice system would come through for her.

Chapter 19

Oakley could not concentrate. Her focus was anywhere except for finishing the storyline in her book. She was worried about Winnie. They had been in touch daily ever since the feds barged into the beach house and whisked Milo away. But now, he was back, and Winnie was taking things day by day with him until a court date was set. Oakley was confident that this was a way for Winnie to end her marriage and keep her child.

Adding to her distraction, Oakley was working at Harper Publishing today. Jack suggested a change of scenery might trigger her imagination and help the words flow onto the page. Being at the office hadn't worked, as she stared at a blinking cursor on a blank page most of the day.

"I need to go home," Oakley blurted out from where she was sitting behind Jack's desk. He looked up at her from the conference table where he had potential book cover layouts scattered across it.

"You want to go back to Edenton?" That caught him off guard. Having her living with him lately could not have felt more perfect. *Seeing her things randomly placed all throughout the house. Sharing meals with her. Having her in his bed every single night.* Jack wasn't ready to give up the normalcy of any of that.

"Well, yeah, eventually," she stated. "I actually just meant your place."

Jack grinned. "But you said, home... your exact words were, I need to go home."

She smiled back at him. "Right. It does feel like home to me."

"It feels pretty good having you there." Jack walked over to his desk and wrapped Oakley in his arms. "Everything about us feels right." They held onto each other tightly and Oakley momentarily closed her eyes. Her life felt complete. She had never been happier or more content. "Go on, take my car. I'll call you later to pick me up and maybe we can grab some dinner?"

"I'd like that," she kissed him on the lips.

He handed her the car keys, and the last words he spoke to her were, "Be safe. I love you."

Oakley took the elevator down to the lobby. At various times throughout the day, there was a hustle and bustle of people. Right now, it was sparse; even the lobby's receptionist desk was vacant. That area was positioned front and center and near the main door in order for a receptionist to be available to anyone who needed directions or guidance. The high-rise had 11 floors, and Harper Publishing was housed on the very top.

Oakley's heels echoed on the marble flooring. She was almost to the main glass doors when someone forcefully pushed one of those doors open and barged in from outside. She backed up.

"You just come and go around here like you own the place!" He slurred his words, and he reeked of alcohol. This was what her mother told her about.

He started drinking. He said he just needed something to take the edge off. It got out of hand, Oakley. I didn't want you exposed to that, and I also wanted to save myself from going down that dark hole with him.

"You shouldn't be here," Oakley told him.

"Why would you say something like that to me? I belong here. I have just as much right to be here as you do!" He wasn't making any sense, and Oakley actually felt unsafe, alone with him in his drunken state. "You can't make me leave, Sondra."

He had her confused with her mother.

"I'm Oakley."

"Nooooo yourrrr're not. Oakley is a little girl," he gestured his hand low to the ground. "Myyyy girl. No one can make me leave her. Not even you, Sandy." She didn't know that her father ever had a nickname for her mother. Perhaps four years old was too young to remember everything.

CONSEQUENCES

"She was a little girl, and you did leave her!" Oakley stated firmly, mostly because she wanted to shock some sense into him.

She watched how unsteady he was on his feet. She thought about just pushing past him and getting the hell out of there. *Where was security in that building when she needed them? And why was the receptionist's station abandoned!* Oakley willed herself to keep calm.

"Stop messing with my head! I hate you, Sondra! And I fucking hate what you did to our lives!" Now he was talking as if he was aware that he left and he lost his family. But he still had Oakley confused with being his wife.

"Why don't we get you some water, or a cup of coffee so you can sober up." *And reconnect with reality.* Oakley attempted to step away, but he aggressively took ahold of her arm. She was able to tear herself away from him just as abruptly.

"Stop harping on me about my drinking! That's all I ever hear from you. You are the reason I need it to think straight!" Clearly that was false, as he could not have been acting more delusional with too much alcohol in his system.

Oakley glanced to the side and noticed the receptionist was finally on her way back to the main desk, and she suddenly was well aware of the distressful situation. Oakley widened her eyes and nodded her way. *Read my mind. Call security to get my father out of here.*

"Don't ignore me! That's so typical of you to act as if I do not even exist." Oakley had enough. She attempted to walk away, and while she did, she yelled directly at the receptionist who already had the phone pressed against her ear. "Call security now!"

But it was too late for help. And it was as if everything that followed now happened in slow motion. She saw him reach behind his back and a second later he held a revolver in his hand. "I'll stop you from writing me off like I don't matter!" Those were the last words that Oakley heard before she held out both of her hands in front of her and attempted to scream. No sound ever came, as she was hit in the abdomen twice. Two bullets pierced into her and she went down. Her world went black while she felt the most intense physical pain. And it was simply too much to bear.

Chapter 20

Jack looked down at his hands. They were bloodstained. Tears sprung to his eyes as he sat alone in the waiting area of the trauma unit at Norfolk General Hospital. He was in his office when security alerted him get down to the lobby. *Oakley had been shot by her delusional father who was now in police custody.*

Jack never before felt panic and fear like he had when he rushed to get to Oakley and then found her lying there. There was so much blood. He cradled her in his arms and begged her to hold on. When the paramedics arrived, they were unsuccessful at stabilizing Oakley. Jack was ordered to follow behind the ambulance because he kept getting in their way. He wouldn't let up; he couldn't stop pleading for Oakley not to give up.

Too much time had passed with no news. Jack told himself that was a good sign because they were helping her, and she was still alive. He called Baylor the moment he sat down and realized no one else knew what happened to Oakley. Baylor absorbed the news and immediately promised that he and Winnie would be there as fast as they could.

In Oakley's cell phone, Jack also found her mother's contact number. He only tried calling her once, but he was unable to get in touch with her. The last thing he was going to do was leave a voicemail stating that her daughter had been shot. Jack was confident that Oakley would be able to call her mother herself sometime soon.

Jack stood up abruptly when a man old enough to be his father pushed through the swinging double doors that led into the waiting area. He wore aqua blue scrubs with a matching cap.

"You're here for Oakley Marks?"

Jack nodded repeatedly. He couldn't find the right words to ask if she was going to be okay. "Just tell me she's alive."

The doctor responded first with a nod. "We are prepping her for an exploratory laparotomy to determine the location of the injuries."

His language seemed unreal. Oakley was shot more than once, and they had no idea what organs had been hit. "I think I understand what you mean. Exploratory basically is your way of saying you don't know what needs repairing until you get in there. What is laparotomy?"

CONSEQUENCES

"A less invasive way to enter. No large incision, unless this is more emergent than we are seeing."

"So this isn't dire, it's not life or death for Oakley in there?"

"Sir, we are doing all that we can to help her. As of now, it does not look like any major organs were penetrated, but she has lost a considerable amount of blood. That's the most I can tell you." The surgeon started to back away, and Jack respected that it was time for him to stop asking questions. This man had a job to do. *Go, save Oakley. Please just help her.*

Winnie saw the caller ID on her phone and was reluctant to answer Baylor, because Milo was home. He was on the opposite end of the house, so she chanced not being overheard.

"Hey, I can't talk right now. What happened to texting first to be sure I'm alone?" She kept her voice low.

"Win. Listen to me. There's no time. It's Oakley. This is an emergency, and we have to get to Norfolk."

"What happened to her?" Winnie had lived this scene before. One phone call could change her life. The one she received with the horrific news about her parents' car accident had left her feeling numb. They were already gone; dead at the scene. Panic rose in her chest again just now. "Baylor, please tell me she's alive."

"She was shot. We have to get to her. It would be faster if you made the drive here and then I'll get us to Norfolk. I can come get you, but that's more time spent on the road."

"I will be there as soon as I can." She hung up. Without question, Winnie knew she was leaving Nags Head Beach in a matter of minutes. She just had to make a fast decision on what to do with Adler. Sally could help, but that would take up time to get to her.

Winnie called for Milo, and he must have picked up on the fear in her voice, because he came running immediately.

"What's wrong?" She saw him look around for Adler.

"I need your help. I have to get to Oakley. She's in Norfolk and I don't know how or why this happened, but she's been shot."

"What?"

"I know, I mean, I don't know! Please, just help me with Adler. I'm almost two hours away and I don't know how soon I can be back. I would ask Sally, but that's time wasted—"

"Winnie, just go. Adler is my child, too. I can handle her. Trust me." *But she didn't.*

Winnie gave in and she hoped to God she was doing the right thing — because Oakley needed her. Milo didn't ask if she was traveling there alone. If he suspected she would be with Baylor, he understood it was not the time to get into that. Winnie grabbed her purse and her keys as she held onto her phone and left immediately after she said, "I'll call you when I get there."

CONSEQUENCES

She wanted to say, *please take good care of Adler,* but she stopped herself because deep down in her soul she already knew that he would.

Milo replied, "I really hope that Oakley will be alright."

The back door was unlocked at Sally's house. Milo held Adler close and he spoke sweetly to her as he knocked twice. "Let's see what Gram is up to, okay? I know she will be happy to see you." He wasn't so sure about himself. He avoided his grandmother since his arrest, and surprisingly she had not made a point to be seen or heard. Sally likely wanted to put a foot up his ass, as Milo often heard her say when he was growing up.

Sally opened the door and immediately reacted to Adler. She had her smiling and laughing and leaning out of her daddy's arms. Sally happily took her from him. They stepped inside and she spoke first. "Where's Winnie?" Milo never showed up with Adler alone.

"She had an emergency. Her friend Oakley needs her in Norfolk."

"Well I hope everything turns out well." Sally knew the situation had to be dire for Winnie to leave Adler with Milo. It's not like he wasn't a caring and attentive father. It was all the other things.

Alder was down on the floor, already crawling and getting into everything familiar to her at Sally's house. Milo stayed in step with her.

"She's fine," Sally assured him. "She certainly knows her surroundings. I'd say she crawls around here like she owns the place." Sally cackled, and Milo smiled.

"I'm really glad she's going to grow up having you in her life, Gram." He was being sincere, and Sally was touched.

"Well I'm not sure if I have decades left in me, but I certainly hope to see this little lady reach her young adult years. She's quite something, you know. A beautiful soul."

"Let's hope she will always take after her mother."

Sally turned to him. "You really screwed up this time, Milo Thomas."

He looked away because it was difficult to look her in the eye. "I'm well aware of that."

"It was your father, wasn't it? You wanted to please him, so you went along with whatever he asked of you. Why in the Sam hell did you take that gamble with your life — especially once you had another little life to consider? See that little girl there? She looks at you as if you hung the moon. All of that awe and reverence and unconditional love that she has for you will one day be completely gone once she's old enough to know the things you've done."

"Of course I wanted to please my father. There's no other way to be on the receiving end of his love and attention," Milo admitted, and he had never said those words aloud to anyone. But, clearly, Gram knew. "When I had my own child, I swore I wouldn't make her feel like she needed to earn anything from me. I love her and I am proud of her, now and forever. My father never once said those words to me."

"So you're blaming your criminal activity on a rotten upbringing by an uncaring, demanding father and an alcoholic piss-poor excuse for a mother? I wonder what the jury will think about that. I doubt too many of them will sympathize with a grown-ass man's whining."

"I'll let my attorney worry about that," he spoke in a snarky tone.

"Meanwhile we all lose everything — our homes, all of our assets."

"Gram, you won't lose this house. Granddad wasn't a part of anything underhanded."

This was the first confirmation Sally had of that. "That's because he never would have been smart enough to cover his own damn tracks."

"Really, Gram? Why can't you just let a dead man rest in peace?"

"Probably because he doesn't deserve to."

"Right," Milo gave up.

"I want to talk about you," Sally noted. "How much longer until you and my three sons are no longer free men?"

"It could take six months to prepare for a trial."

"And if you're found guilty?"

"Twenty years." Milo's chest felt heavy at the mere thought of it becoming fact.

This came as no surprise to Sally. She only wished it would not be true. "I am incredibly disappointed in all of you, but especially you, Milo Thomas. You had so much potential to not be like them. I saw the good. I told you over and over again that you could be a better man than the rest of them. But, I was wrong. Wishful thinking, I guess. You're just as rotten and self-centered. You're no different. You're not special like I always wanted so desperately to believe. You've treated your wife terribly. No one would blame her if she turned her back on you and bolted the hell out of this town. You held her child over her head, time and again, forcing your wife to stay with you. You played on her goodness and mercy! And now, will you just look at how it all panned out? She is going to have the upper hand; it's only a matter of time. You're going to lose this little girl," Sally glanced at Adler and then back at Milo. He had tears spilling over in his eyes, and he wasn't wiping them off his face as they streamed down his cheeks and dripped off his chin. He was a sloppy, pitiful mess. Sally stopped. She had said enough, and her words were harsh. The reality here was no matter how angry and disappointed she was in her grandson —the one Brand who she adored, faults and all— she could never bring herself to disown him.

Milo bent forward and sunk to his knees on the hardwood flooring. He wouldn't let anyone else see his pain. Only his Gram.

She had a way of reaching him, getting to him, and then being there for him — despite everything.

It took her a moment to slowly get down to her old, knobby knees. Her chronic aching back hindered most movements. But, when Milo lifted his face out of his hands, she was there; and she held onto him with everything she had left to give.

Chapter 21

When Baylor and Winnie finally arrived at Norfolk General Hospital, the waiting area was empty. Their worry was enhanced when Jack didn't answer his cell phone. They knew the story. They were aware that Oakley was shot twice by her father and the injury was in her abdomen. And the last time they had spoken with Jack, he told them Oakley was still in surgery.

"Maybe Oakley is out of surgery and Jack was able to see her," Baylor tried to comfort Winnie and ease his own worry.

"She has to be okay," Winnie fought tears. "Her life was just now coming together in so many ways. It just wouldn't be fair for it to end this way." With that said, they both knew that life wasn't fair. So much had happened in all of their lives to support that fact. Even still, they've always had each other. They were the triplex trio.

CONSEQUENCES

Earlier, the surgeon had returned to the waiting area for Jack. His heart was in his throat as he heard the doctor's words. The significant blood loss that Oakley suffered from had complicated the surgery, but she pulled through it. They discovered that her appendix had been the target that was damaged by both bullets. Oakley had gotten lucky, considering the appendix could easily be removed without further issue. Jack could finally breathe when he heard those words. There was still the concern, though, for Oakley's total blood volume, as she had lost more than thirty percent. Following surgery, her blood pressure dropped as her heart rate increased and her breathing became shallow. She was being monitored very closely and would likely need a blood transfusion. Jack didn't know if they shared a compatible blood type, but he swore he would give her every last drop of his own if it meant her life would be saved. He asked to see her, and the doctor allowed him.

She was still heavily sedated from the surgery when Jack sat near her bedside. She looked no different to him, other than her face had lost its color. Even pale, she had the most beautiful face. He gently touched his fingers to the soft skin on her cheek. "Thank you for fighting so hard. I need you more than you'll ever know, but you can be sure that I am going to spend the rest of my life telling you just how much. Please don't ever scare me like that again, Oak."

He watched her eyes slowly open, and she attempted to curve her lips to form a smile. But then her heavy eyelids closed again. She was too weak and exhausted from the trauma to her body, but Oakley managed to let Jack know that she heard his every word. "You just rest. I will be right here."

A short while later, Jack stepped away to give Baylor and Winnie the good news. The moment he entered the waiting area, they saw him, and Winnie immediately began to cry. Jack reached for her hand and held it. "She pulled through!" he could hardly contain his excitement. "Her appendix was hit and had to be removed. She lost a lot of blood and may need a transfusion, but all she has to do now is heal." Baylor wrapped his arm around Winnie, and she was still holding Jack's hand. "You love her as much as we do," Winnie noted, when she watched Jack wipe away his tears.

"More than anything," he spoke genuinely to Oakley's best friends. "She's going to be so touched that you two are here."

Two days later, Oakley had a visit from her mother. Sondra Marks was furious that her daughter's life could have been taken by her own father. There was something she said in her fit of rage that weighed on Oakley's mind.

"Where is my father?" Oakley asked Jack, who had been making himself feel at home in her hospital room. He sat beside her bed with his legs crossed at the knee, balancing a laptop. He had work to do, but he was not about to leave that hospital without Oakley. He only went home once daily to shower and change clothes. Oakley was touched by everything he had said and done for her, but she reassured him that she was going to be fine. Right now, though, she needed to know the details about her father. How long was he going to be in police custody? Her mother had demanded that she press charges and put him in prison for the rest of his miserable life.

"He's in jail."

"For how long?"

"Well, honestly, that's going to be up to you, Oak."

"My mother expects me to press charges."

"I hope that you do. I don't want him anywhere near you ever again. He's unstable. He could have killed you. I can't take knowing that he could try again."

"I want to see him."

"How?"

Jack watched her reach for her cell phone. She searched online for the contact information for the Norfolk Police Department. She dialed the number and asked for the commanding chief. Oakley was a woman who took charge. She didn't answer to anyone or ask for help too often. That's what Jack loved most about her. Her independence was admirable and sexy. He was, however, apprehensive about Oakley's request to have Trey Marks brought to her hospital room.

There were two conditions. One, an officer of the law would escort her father into her hospital room and then stand guard directly outside of the door. And two, Jack was allowed to stay after he insisted and Oakley agreed. Truth be told, she was haunted by the fact that her father harmed her and the idea of being alone with him again was never going to happen. Not if she had her way today.

Jack stood near the window when the officer brought *the prisoner* into the room. Oakley could feel her heart pounding in her chest. He wasn't wearing an orange jumpsuit as she imagined, just a t-shirt and jeans. His hands were cuffed in front of his body, and she noticed his gray hair was cropped shorter.

Oakley forced herself to make eye contact with him, even though she was trembling inside. She didn't look over at Jack, but she could feel his eyes on her.

"I'm sure you're wondering why I asked to see you," Oakley began, and her father lifted his eyes from the floor to her.

"I'll never forgive myself for hurting you. I was out of my mind. You have to know that I never would shoot my own daughter."

"But you did," she spoke through clenched teeth. "You robbed me of my childhood all those years ago when you abandoned me, and then you came back and tried to end my life."

"I'm going to get clean and sober. No more drugs or alcohol. I want to be a better man."

"Good for you," Oakley's words were callous, and insincere.

CONSEQUENCES

"I know I'm looking at prison time, and you have every right to press charges against me. I deserve what's coming to me. But I want the chance to prove to you that I can be a good father. Don't give up on me now."

"Give up on you?" Oakley raised her voice and moved too quickly on the bed, which ricocheted a sharp pain through her abdomen. She flinched, and Jack had his eye on her. He wanted to tell her to take it easy, but he promised he would be a silent bystander in the room. And he couldn't justify telling her to calm down when that man standing there was a monster, who deserved to be on the receiving end of her anger. "I gave up on you a long time ago. I had to, in order to survive the disappointment of you leaving me. And, yes, I was told that I have the ability to lock you up for a long time. The thing about that is, I don't want to." Both her father and Jack stared at her in disbelief. "I don't want to have it hanging over my head for the rest of my life, that I took away your freedom. No," she shook her head, "I want the freedom to choose here. What I want is for you to be gone from my life. Leave, and never come back, just as you did when I was a child. I can't live with looking over my shoulder, wondering if you are going to just randomly show up and shoot me."

"I don't understand," her father's voice quivered. It was obvious that he was expecting to serve his prison time and earn his daughter's forgiveness — maybe even eventually a place in her life again.

"It's as simple as I am not going to press charges against my own father. You are free to go, but I never want to see you again. Stay out of my life and out of my sight."

He was deeply affected by her words. He looked down at his feet and broke into a sob. Jack watched Oakley keep her own composure intact.

"I'll need your word on my offer. If you cannot promise that you will leave me the hell alone, I will press charges to force you to stay away."

Her father raised his head and cleared his throat. "Either way, I lose you."

"You lost me when I was four years old and you made the choice not to turn back when I begged you to stay." Oakley fought the urge to become emotional. That memory would always haunt her.

"If that is what you want, I will leave."

Oakley watched him turn on his heels. She silently choked on a sob just as he spun back around to face her. "I'll always be proud of my little girl."

Jack stepped forward this time, and with a firm nudge, he walked Oakley's father all the way to the door.

Once Jack closed the door, Oakley fell apart. Tears were streaming down her face and her arms were folded tightly across her abdomen. "That was so hard," she cried.

He made his way over to her and gently enveloped her in his arms. "I've got you. Just let it out."

"I thought you would be upset that I decided not to press charges."

CONSEQUENCES

He shook his head. "The woman I fell in love with calls the shots. It's how she survives. I get that."

She smiled at him through her tears.

In an odd way, her life had come full circle today. She always carried abandonment in her soul. She failed to make her daddy stay. No matter how hard she tried to erase it, the pain of that truth was always there. She was the little girl who was left. Decades later, she drew strength and courage from that same pain — to be the one to make him leave. There was an undeniable sense of peace in her soul now.

Chapter 22

Most people live their lives believing that there will always be time. Milo thought that he had six months of freedom, until he received the unexpected call from his attorney eight weeks later. He, along with his father and his uncles, deliberated for days about what was being asked of them. A plea bargain was on the table and up for grabs. If they pled guilty to multiple counts of money laundering and drug trafficking, a trial would be waived, and lesser sentencings could be served. Less than twenty years naturally appealed to all of them, so eventually they agreed to relinquish their right to a fair trial by judge and jury in a court of law. There was a downside, though. A trial often took months to prepare for, and several weeks once it began. Without one, a sentencing date would be set, and prison time would immediately follow. Milo wasn't prepared to leave his wife and baby. *How does anyone prepare themselves for a goodbye like that?*

CONSEQUENCES

On the morning of the hearing, Milo wore a dark suit with a yellow tie. Winnie caught herself remembering the first time she ever saw him, getting out of his vehicle in front of Sally's house. He wore that same suit and yellow tie. He looked dapper then and still now. She remembered how he charmed her, and almost instantly had an inexplicable hold over her. Winnie, oddly, had mixed emotions about this day. It was her husband's day of reckoning, and her chance to finally be free of him.

She saw him sit down on the sofa in the living room where Adler was watching her favorite Disney cartoon. He didn't have her attention, but he took advantage of that time to just be near her. Winnie could only imagine what was going through his mind. What he was feeling had been her greatest fear. *Being forced to leave her baby.*

"Will Gram watch Adler this morning?"

"No," Winnie replied. "She's going to be in the courtroom." There was a family, who lived near them on the beach, that Winnie had gotten to know. They had twin teenage daughters, who offered to babysit Adler anytime. Today she called on them for help. "The Wilken twins are going to come over for awhile and play with her." Milo didn't respond. He was thinking how all the decisions from this moment forward, that pertained to Adler Jo, would now be made solely by Winnie. It was as if his role as an active father was now null and void.

While they were talking, Adler left her spot on the floor and made her way onto the sofa to be near her daddy. Milo pulled her close and tucked her under his arm. Winnie looked away. She wasn't sure that she could handle witnessing this.

"You are the best baby girl that a daddy could ever wish for, do you know that?" Adler babbled something and added her typical Dada chant at the end. "That's right. I'm your daddy, and I love you so much. I am very proud to call you mine. Daddy needs to go away for a little while, but I will see you soon," Milo glanced at Winnie. Her expression didn't falter. She was sad but holding herself together.

"Bye-bye," Adler spoke as if her words were on cue.

"Yes, see, you are so smart. Daddy has to go bye-bye, but I will see you soon, okay?" Milo's voice cracked. Winnie watched him pick her up and hold her close. He kissed her face, her hair, and her face again. And the last thing he said to her was, "Daddy loves you more than anything."

Milo then placed her on the floor, and with slumped shoulders he walked out of the beach house without looking back.

A few minutes later, the twins next door arrived and Winnie spent a few minutes walking them through the house and giving them instructions for taking care of Adler. Once she left, she found Milo sitting in her Jeep waiting.

"Before we leave," he said, as she turned over the engine, "there's something that I want to say to you."

Here we go, Winnie thought. *Here come the demands, the threats to disown them, and the typical Milo way of controlling her. Even from behind bars.*

CONSEQUENCES

"In my office, there are documents on top of my desk. I've already signed them, and if you choose to sign them, they must be filed for us to be legally divorced." Winnie again forced herself to remain expressionless. "I'm saving you the trouble, because I know that's what you want; what you've wanted all along. I know you are going to run to him." She thought of Baylor and that moment. "I'm going to face years in prison, I've accepted that. I guess it really doesn't matter how long. The only thing I need is for you to allow me to see my daughter. Divorce me. Start your fairytale life with him. Just don't keep Adler from me. Please."

She was speechless. She realized the time was now or never. Milo really didn't deserve to know if she had made a final decision about allowing Alder to be in his life, but Winnie owed it to herself to honor the person she was before she became Mrs. Milo Brand. She once believed that everyone deserved a second chance. She wasn't naïve though. Milo had put her through pure hell. She was done with him. She wanted her freedom and she was going to take it and run. But she would see to it that her daughter would grow up knowing her father. She wouldn't be the one responsible for severing their special bond. You see, Winnie had already thought this through. Sally was going to be their middle person. Her visits to Milo in prison would include Adler. Winnie, for now, wanted no part of it.

"Just consider it, okay?" Milo could no longer take her silence. *Dammit. Was she going to take his daughter away from him, or not?*

"You've taken so much from me," she told him. "I owe you nothing, but our innocent daughter should not have to suffer because of your mistakes and my anguish." She paused. "I will make sure that Adler stays in contact with you. You have my word."

Milo's face lit up as if he was just told his prison sentencing was canceled. "I don't know how to thank you, Wynette."

"Don't. I don't want your gratitude or anything else. Just be who our daughter needs you to be."

Winnie shifted the Jeep into reverse, backed out, and then drove off to the federal courthouse.

Winnie sat close to Sally in the courtroom. The other three Brand women were seated together in a different row of chairs. Milo and his two uncles were present with their lawyers, but Thomas Brand was absent and said to have fallen ill just hours ago. Winnie kept quiet about what Milo told her. *His father vowed to take his own life before he would ever allow them to lock him up.*

The hearing began with the judge's stern words. "We can't allow our banks to be laundromats for cartel cash. Once respectable bank owners, such as all of you, who laundered drug money for traffickers, will face prosecution and prison. There will be no way around that; and given a guilty plea from each of you, I will now begin ordering fines, seizing of assets, and sentencing.

CONSEQUENCES

Winnie took a deep breath, as she looked down at Sally's aged hands that were tightly clasped together on her lap. She was the matriarch of this family; a family whose downfall would forever affect so many lives. Sally thought of all her grandchildren and her one great granddaughter. How unfair for them. Their legacy was forever tarnished.

By the time the judge was done speaking, Winnie's chest felt heavy. She had her arm tightly around Sally, who was holding up well; she was indeed a pilar of strength.

Milo, his father, and his uncles were each fined $500,000. The judge also ruled that upon the death of any of the defendants, as well as their wives, they will be required to surrender their remaining assets in order to settle the remaining claims. That would inevitably cancel out any trusts upon death for grandchildren or great grandchildren. Brand First National Bank would stay open, but at this point it was unclear if any of the Brands were going to own and operate it. It was also noted that both Sally and Remi's stock in Brand First National Bank was legit. Their money was clean, so their assets would be left untouched. It was obvious then that the Brand men had protected them. With that mentioned, Sally dabbed her eyes with a wadded tissue in her hand.

And finally, all the Brand men were individually sentenced to 18 years in the state penitentiary.

Chapter 23

Winnie followed Sally home to be sure she arrived safely. She also didn't want her to be alone at a time like this.

The two of them sat at the kitchen table, drinking coffee with a shot of Baileys Irish Cream. Sally insisted the liqueur would calm their nerves.

"I'm really happy to know that your fortune, and Remi's, is legit money and safe from the court's seizing. And your home, too, Sally. That was one of my greatest worries for you." None of them had any idea how deep the dirty money was hidden.

Sally nodded. "I am grateful, but I must say I'm feeling a little lost. What does this home mean to me anymore? It may be ample time for me to consider selling and downsizing to something a little easier on my knees and back." Her broken heart that held the memories of raising her children in that house just didn't feel the same.

CONSEQUENCES

"You don't have to make a rash decision now," Winnie advised her. "Let the shock wear off first."

Sally agreed. "What about you, honey? What does today's events mean for you and little Adler? How will you raise her in the beach house that brought you so much misery?" It appeared as if Sally had already read her mind. Winnie could not stay there.

"I don't want Milo's fortune. I have no interest in spending his money to raise my daughter. I will accept an already-implemented trust for Adler now, instead of when she turns 18 years old, but that is all. I will move back to Edenton and raise her on Orion Lane. It only feels right, Sally. I hope you aren't too disappointed."

"Disappointed? I'm overjoyed for you! You once made that 40-mile commute to me practically daily and I expect that to continue." Sally couldn't bear to lose anyone else in her life.

"You know that will never change," Winnie reassured her.

Sally patted her hand from across the table. "Drink up, and get going. I'm sure your Baylor is waiting to welcome you home."

No words had ever sounded sweeter.

Winnie had already texted him from her car outside of the courthouse. Baylor knew it was over. Milo could no longer claim, nor control Winnie. The day he was locked up was the day Winnie was set free.

Once Winnie was back at the beach house and alone with Adler, she began to pack up their things. Just a few days' worth of clothes and belongings. She called Baylor after she loaded her Jeep.

"Hey," she spoke to him.

"I can't stop smiling," he told her.

She laughed out loud. "I'm happy, too. It's strange because it doesn't feel real to me yet. The only thing I know for sure is that I don't want to spend another night in this house."

"Then come home, Win."

Winnie blinked through the tears in her eyes. "Say it again, please."

"It's time for you to move back home where you can feel at peace with your life. None of what has happened matters anymore. Come watch the sunset with me on the pier, and let me hold you while we count our lucky stars in the sky."

Winnie told herself this wasn't a dream anymore. It was the reality that her dream had finally come true.

Between the news coverage and the updates from Winnie and Baylor, Oakley was well informed in Norfolk. She was mostly recovered, but she had not been back to the triplex in well over two months. Knowing that Winnie and Adler were in the process of moving back there for good, Oakley knew she had to break it to Jack that she wanted to be there again, to at least be a part of their homecoming.

Oakley was in the conference room at Harper Publishing, where Jack asked her to meet him. She knew what was going on. Her second book was nearing publication; she had finished writing it at Jack's condo while recovering from her injuries. Her contract with Harper Publishing was about to expire. She feared that Jack would attempt to talk to her into renewing it. Or perhaps to write another book, a single read this time with all new characters and setting. Oakley's mind was made up. She was finished with publishing contracts and writing books for awhile. *Maybe forever.*

Jack closed the door behind him. He carried a stack of papers in his hand.

"Wait. Don't say a word about what you're carrying with you there," she stated, sort of smiling. "Today is don't bind me to another contract day!"

Jack chuckled. "Actually, we've been over this. I respect your decision; I really do. These are your parting papers. Read over them carefully, sign that you agree, and you will be free to walk out of here."

"No more obligations, right?"

"Read, Oakley."

"Yes, Jack."

It was all typical. Her royalties were listed for Book 1 and were now expected to at least double with Book 2. Her contract with Harper Publishing had expired and it was understood that it was her wish not to renew it.

And then there was one final paragraph at the bottom.

It read:

Take note that it's been several months since you were made aware that once your contract expired with my company, I would confidently place another offer on the table. Answer me this, Oakley Marks… What are you doing for the rest of your life?

She looked up from reading. He was sitting close to her and his eyes bore into hers, as he anxiously waited for her answer. Her smile met her eyes. "I can't imagine my life without you."

"Don't keep me in suspense. What are you doing for the rest of forever, Oakley?"

"Spending it with you, because I am going to marry you, Jack."

He pulled her close and kissed her hard and full on the mouth.

"I think I better take you home so we can celebrate," Jack noted, touching her.

"Home. Can we talk about where our home will be?" This made her nervous. She still doubted that Jack truly understood her emotional pull to Orion Lane, and to Winnie and Baylor.

CONSEQUENCES

"I have a suggestion," Jack offered. "How would you feel about having a weekend home?"

"The triplex?"

Jack nodded. "We could pack up early every Friday afternoon and not come back until late on Sundays. It will be the best of both worlds, I hope. It's the only way I could come up with where neither one of us will have to give up our homes, our lives as we know it. The bottom line is—"

"What about my bottom?" she interrupted him.

"It's cute, it has the perfect roundness; super sexy," he grabbed her buttocks with both of his hands and pulled her close to him. "As I was saying before you inappropriately interrupted me, what's most important is that we are together. I don't want to live apart or sleep apart ever again for the rest of our lives."

"That sounds like a binding offer," Oakley winked.

"One that will never expire," Jack promised.

He kissed her and she lost herself in him.

Chapter 24

She knew that houses in Nags Head Beach could be on the market for several months, sometimes a year or more, before they sold. That was not the case for Sally's seventy-something-year-old vintage home near the beach. And just like that she was moving to a smaller, one-level, quaint cottage only two miles away. The beach wasn't in her backyard anymore, but it was within walking distance.

Sally sent Winnie to follow the moving truck to her new cottage. There was one last thing she needed to do, alone. She sat down on the swing near her rose garden. The swing was special, too, but she never told anyone why. It was a two-seater wooden bench swing. Remington Boyd made it for her, and there was an inscription underneath. *Slowly and steadily, let this swing carry you back to me in your daydreams.*

Throughout their affair, the two of them had never been able to spend a night together; they had only been daytime lovers.

Sally folded her arms across her chest and closed her eyes. She could still feel him there with her sometimes.

CONSEQUENCES

A voice startled her back to reality when her eyes popped open. "I had to see for myself that you're really leaving this house and your beloved rose garden behind." Remi closed the space between them and reached for her mother's hand.

"You came after all," Sally's sadness subsided knowing that Remi was there to help her say goodbye. Only she and Winnie knew the truth behind all the memories there.

"Scoot," Remi told her, and then she sat down close to her mother.

"Where've you been all these months?" Remi knew exactly what Sally was getting at.

"Indianola Valley in Utah. It's beautiful there. I'm staying in a pioneer house on the grounds of the most peaceful ranch in the world."

Sally stared at her for a long while before she spoke. "He was there once, wasn't he?"

Remi nodded. "There's a rose garden just like yours. It's decades old, but still flourishing. And, there's a swing in the distance that hangs from a 100-year-old maple tree. It's handmade with two braided ropes and a board seat."

"Is there an inscription?" Sally asked with bated breath.

"Is there one on this swing, Mom?"

Sally nodded. "Yes, underneath. It's handwritten. Slowly and steadily, let this swing carry you back to me in your daydreams." Those words would always be beautiful to her.

"Remi, what does it say on the bottom of that swing at that ranch?"

"Just one word," she answered. "Daydreams."

A sob caught in Sally's throat and she brought her hand to her lips. Remi reached for her, wrapping her up in comfort and love. And when Sally caught her breath again, she spoke. "He's gone, isn't he?"

Remi's eyes were clouded with tears when she looked directly at Sally. "Yes."

"Do you know how or when?"

"Eight years ago. His heart gave out. He was found on the grounds of the ranch."

A tear streamed down Sally's cheek. She left it there as she gazed up at the sky. "I never stopped loving him."

"I think I can say the same for him not being able to forget you either," Remi's words were genuine.

"Do something for me."

"I'll certainly try, Mom."

"When you find the truest kind of love and happiness in your life, don't give it up for anything."

Remi smiled. That's why she was going back to the ranch.

In Indianola Valley, Nina led Remi to the right people. There was an elderly man who lived in an assisted living center in Fairview. He had been another hired hand on the ranch who worked side by side Remington Boyd. His name was Ford. The day that Remi had visited him, looking for answers about her birthfather, she discovered that he and her father were once best friends. Remi stayed for hours talking to him. He still had a sharp mind and a good memory. He was the one who told her to flip over that swing and read the message. He knew it was meant for a woman that Remington had in his heart, because whenever anyone asked him why he had never married, he would always reply the same, *"My heart is in North Carolina."* Ford also had a grandson named after him. He had the bluest eyes, broadest shoulders, and waviest brown hair. His hands were that of a hard-working rancher. Calloused, but as soft and gentle as silk when he touched her. For the first time in her life, Remi had a reason to settle down somewhere.

"Will you let me take you there?" Remi asked Sally. "There's so much more that I want to tell you and show you."

Sally imagined she would say yes to Remi's offer very soon. "Thank you for finding where he ended up. I've always wondered if he was content with his life."

"I believe that he was." Remi only wished that she would have been able to meet him. Instead, he had given her a gift. Meeting his best friend had led her to a man who could very well be her soul mate.

Sally crossed her arms over her chest and started to move the swing with her feet. Remi assisted, slowly and steadily, while they both got carried away daydreaming.

Chapter 25

Six months later, Winnie was lathering sunscreen on Adler. She wouldn't stand still long enough for anything because, like most 15-month-olds, she was on the go all the time. "Bay?" she asked, and Winnie's smile lit up her face. "Yes, Baylor is outside, and we are going to go see him."

The triplex on Orion Lane was Winnie's home again. She and Baylor were raising Adler together, while sharing both her unit and his. They joked that they should just knock down the wall between the two places to have more living space. Nothing was keeping them apart anymore, and Winnie was happier than she had ever been in her entire life. She allowed Adler to visit Milo in prison every weekend with Sally. Winnie never asked how he was doing or if he was coping, and Sally only commented on the things that pertained to both Milo and Adler. Winnie was gradually gaining momentum with new clients as she had restarted her caretaker business in Nags Head Beach. She was cleaning five houses a week, grocery shopping for several elderly folks, and she still worked for Sally on a daily basis. Winnie was doing alright financially. In the divorce settlement, she accepted the trust in Adler's name. Winnie also sold the beach house and agreed to take her half of the profit. That money served as a cushion in her bank account. Everything else, she left for Milo — who wouldn't have a need for it for almost two decades, unless he was released from prison early for good behavior. None of that concerned Winnie. She had a new life to live now.

CONSEQUENCES

The front door swung open and Oakley barged in with Jack on her heels. Adler immediately stopped playing and ran into Jack's arms. He bent down to catch her the moment she was at his feet. Oakley threw her hands up in the air. "Gee thanks, Harper. I used to be her favorite." Winnie laughed. Having the two of them at the triplex every weekend was wonderful. She knew how special it was for them to be in Adler's life.

"I saw Baylor getting the pontoon ready," Jack noted. "We're all set. Mind if I take Adler out there with me?" Jack asked Winnie.

"Sure, go ahead. Take her hat, and don't let her down on the pier unless you plan to be ready to dive in after her." They laughed.

Oakley smiled at Winnie when Jack walked away holding Adler. "He's so good with her."

"Good thing, as one day he will be your baby daddy." They giggled.

"Ah," Oakley sighed. "Look at us. Our lives are so different now, but complete in ways that we never saw coming."

Winnie nodded. "We've finally grown up."

"I have something to tell you," Oakley stepped closer, as if she was going to whisper a secret in her ear. "I got a job."

"As in a real job where you actually work and earn a paycheck?"

Oakley shoved her shoulder. "Not exactly. I'm volunteering at the women's shelter in Norfolk. I stopped in there a few weeks ago to leave a donation to help out the women and children who end up there because they are homeless or abandoned. I got caught up in what I saw there. Those children don't deserve to feel lost and alone."

"Awe, Oak, you found a connection to them."

"I did, Oakley nodded, "and I want to help them. I don't know, I can listen and hold them and just make them feel strong again. I want them to believe that they are going to be okay."

"I am so proud of you," Winnie beamed. "On the surface, I think you were always perceived as the spoiled rich girl, and that you were in many ways, but knowing you and loving you opened my eyes to the fact that everyone has their own pain. You were just really good at concealing yours."

"It's not a healthy way to survive," Oakley noted. "That's why I want to help at the shelter in any way that I can. I realized, when I stepped inside that place, that I wanted to do more than just write out a check and leave."

"And here you thought all along that being a writer was your destiny."

"No. Being a writer was what led me to Jack."

They both smiled.

"Let's go see how the boys are handling Adler out there," Winnie turned to look out the patio door. She would never tire of seeing that view of the pier overlooking the bay.

CONSEQUENCES

"First, take a minute to check your calendar. We only have two months to find you a maid of honor dress, and I know how you are about shopping, so let me pick it out for you. All you have to do is be there for the fitting."

Winnie's expression changed, and Oakley only assumed it was because she highly disliked shopping. She was long past her struggle with bulimia and was a healthy, curvaceous woman again. "I think we better wait until the wedding date gets a little closer for my try-on."

Oakley was about to roll her eyes when Winnie pulled back the cover-up for her swimsuit to reveal a perfectly round pooch.

Oakley squealed, "You've got a little Baylor in there!"

Winnie was beaming. "We are so happy to be together, raising Adler, and now we're going to have a baby to complete our family."

Just then, Baylor stepped through the patio door entrance. "Hey, you two—" he looked from one to the other. His two best friends in the entire word. He cherished them both endlessly. He could also read their faces anytime regarding anything. "You told Oak our news..."

Oakley took three giant strides with her long legs and wrapped her arms around Baylor's neck. He pulled her close and kissed the top of her head. Winnie stood close and Baylor reached for her as well.

The patio door was open as a warm spring breeze made its way inside. They turned to admire the view of another perfect day on Orion Lane.

Their lives had not always been peaceful, and they did not expect to never again face trials. But, for them, peace did not mean to be in a place where there was no trouble or commotion. It meant to sometimes be in the midst of things both good and bad — and still be calm in their hearts. Winnie, Baylor, and Oakley had finally found their calm.

About the Author

For me, the most enjoyable part of writing a trilogy is being able to continue a storyline throughout three books with the same characters in an already established setting. At the close of one book, I am able to pick up right where I left off for the beginning of the next book. It's effortless writing when I'm already attached to the characters — and Winnie, Baylor, and Oakley certainly have a piece of my heart in the fictional world.

From Book 1 (Vulnerability) to Book 2 (High Standards), the lives of the trio from the triplex significantly changed, and finally evolved in Book 3 (Consequences).

Winnie's character undoubtedly experienced the most growth. She became a mother and suddenly had someone else to love and protect — and to sacrifice everything for. Milo's presence in her life changed her in ways she was not proud of, as he had the power to make her feel weak and desperate at times. Her story with Milo came full circle by the end of Book 3 when she had the upper hand in their marriage. She unexpectedly held power. But it was only fitting for Winnie's true, righteous self to emerge at the end of this story when she chose to do the right thing for her daughter.

Like Winnie's character, sometimes we all believe that we need other people to tell us what's good, what's bad, or what we should be doing. When, really, we have to power to make up our own mind, and to be accountable to ourselves in this world. Own your life. Personal failures should be because you made the choice, not because anyone else decided for you.

As always, thank you for reading!

love,

Lori Bell